SEARCHING

WHEN SONGBIRDS CEASED TO SING

Jean A. Quaal

"Passed years seem safe ones, vanquished ones, while the future lives in a cloud, formidable from a distance. The cloud clears as you enter it." ~ Beryl Markha

Searching, When Songbirds Ceased to Sing

Copyright © 2025 *Jean A. Quaal*

ISBN (Paperback): 979-8-89672-212-0
ISBN (Hardback): 979-8-89672-213-7
ISBN (Ebook): 979-8-89672-214-4

All rights reserved. No part of this book may be used or reproduced by any means, graphic, electronic, or mechanical, including photocopying, recording, taping or by information storage and retrieval system without the written permission of the author except in the case of brief quotations embodied in critical articles and reviews.

Because of the dynamic nature of the Internet, any web addresses or links contained in this book may have changed since publication and may no longer be valid. The views expressed in the work are solely those of the author and do not necessarily reflect the views of the publisher, and the publisher hereby disclaims any responsibility for them.

Printed in the United States of America.

PROMINENT
BOOKS
EDGE

5830 E 2nd St, Ste 7000 #9983
Casper, WY 82609
USA

CONTENTS

AUTHORS NOTE

At some time or another, everyone has searched for something. Who, amongst us, has not reached sheer frustration when trying to locate car keys, eyeglasses, or an elusive TV remote control most likely hiding beneath a couch cushion! In today's fast-paced world, cellphones, iPods, tablets, and laptops are considered vital necessities that control our daily lives. This is realized when we misplace any one of them.

But, what if; the something… is someone! That's when, *'things'* deemed vitally important become unimportant, when something seemingly significant becomes insignificant, when frustration defies description. For those who have dealt with the torment of searching for a missing loved one, I extend my sincere compassion and deepest empathy.

"Searching, When Songbirds Ceased to Sing" shares the hows, whys and whats; that evolved during a traumatic year-long search -- not for one, but for five someones! Intertwined throughout the story are shared memories from a secure past. Backtracking in time served as an invaluable coping tool when faced with daily uncertainty, helplessness, apprehension, and fear of the unknown.

INTRODUCTION

It was fall of 1974, October 28th when my husband and his brother-in-law, piloting Beechcraft Baron 414K, disappeared. The aircraft, serving as an air hearse, was on a return flight from Gallup, New Mexico. A father and his two teenage daughters involved in a fatal car/train accident were being transported to their hometown of Sturgis, South Dakota for burial.

When failing to arrive at the Sturgis Airport as scheduled, Rapid City Flight Service issued a Missing Aircraft Alert to all surrounding airports. With no sightings or landings reported, the alert broadened to include all airports in a six-state area, and an extensive air search immediately commenced. The initial shock of the airplane's sudden disappearance was beyond devastating for the occupants' families whose lives were forever altered.

Autumn had already established itself as my least favorite time of year long before, since childhood when school functions and birthday parties were cancelled due to early snowstorms. Granted the season is dazzling, spectacular at its peak. It presents itself as a shimmering pot of glittering gold filled with emerald and ruby gems, but its finale is an unsightly scene, comparable to a corroded beat-up rusty burn-barrel of charred tin cans and ashes. Wilting flowers struggle, fight cold bitter nights; droopy trees brood bare branches as rotting fruit lay atop brittle, decayed leaves below. Tell me, who doesn't feel a tinge of sadness when overhead wedges of honking geese bid farewell; when silence drowns out cheerful calls that echoed across misty meadows; when emptiness consumes the autumn air as musical medleys sounding from tall treetops stop, when songbirds cease to sing!

The season encourages human migration to more welcoming environments—the same as our feathered friends. People change things, when we can: homes, jobs, vehicles, laws, schools, and our minds! Unfortunately, try as we may, there are two things that no amount of 'want to' can change; the weather and something that has already happened. This story is about something that happened which uprooted lives, reinforcing my unfavorable assessment of autumn, which thereafter became a foreboding time met with apprehension.

CHAPTER 1

Business Beginnings

Hlavka Flying Service began in 1964, from a row of old wooden tin-covered hangers located at the Municipal Airport, six miles east of Sturgis, South Dakota. Roger purchased the open-front, four-sectioned shed and his first plane from Harold Johnstone, best known as '*Johnny*' who served in the US Navy during World War II as a naval aviator in the Pacific, and taught Roger everything he knew about flying an airplane, including how to spray crops and control coyotes. Shortly after earning his instructor's rating, during off-time from duties as newly appointed Meade County Deputy Sheriff, Roger began touring the countryside giving lessons in his prized beauty—a bright yellow 1946 Super Club.

Roger Hlavka and Johnny Johnstone

The north end of the dated structure was converted into an office, with a bathroom and lobby area which served as a ground school classroom, as well. The southern two hangers housed the J-3 and Pawnee spray plane. We engaged the assistance of Ivan Ellis, a respected, highly regarded aircraft mechanic recently retired from Busfield Aviation at Belle Fourche, South Dakota. Ivan organized the middle section of the shed into a maintenance shop. Shortly after joining us, he was chosen by the FAA as South Dakota's Mechanic of the Year for his lifetime contribution to aviation safety.

That was in 1971, the same year Jerry Burnham, friend and local auto mechanic was offered a deal that couldn't be refused. With Roger's financial assistance and the chance to work under the best mechanic in the country, Jerry attended Cannon Aeronautical School in Cheyenne, Wyoming where he obtained his Aircraft Maintenance licenses, private pilot's license and became our second full-time aircraft mechanic.

Original Hangers and Hlavka Flying Service Office

Eddie Hlavka, Bonnie Chapman, Jean Hlavka, Lorie Hlavka

After five years of serving as Meade County Deputy Sheriff, Roger left law enforcement to assume the Sturgis Airport Manager position. He immediately began working with city officials to improve the outdated dirt strip into a lengthy, well-lit paved runway and signed an agreement to construct our new buildings on city property. By this time, he had acquired his commercial and multi-engine ratings, and established charter contracts with Sturgis Community Memorial and Fort Meade Veterans Hospital.

Our business was renamed Hlavka Aviation, Inc., and expanded into a full service FBO offering flight instruction, crop spraying, air ambulance, charter service, aircraft sales, and maintenance. Through sheer determination, willpower, grit and gaining the confidence of our local banker; we were granted a substantial line of credit, and established floor plan financial programs with Bellanca and Cessna Aircraft Corporations.

As things progressed and skyways took preference over highways, as our main means of transit; realizing my knowledge of small aircraft required attention, I began taking flying lessons. My interests were not to be the first female crop duster in the area, perform daring aerial acrobatics, or haul passengers. Frankly, I was not that crazy about flying but wanted the assurance of knowing how to safely maneuver a plane out of airspace and back onto solid ground…if, ever had to!

The day I soloed came as a complete surprise. Having acquired only eight hours flying time with Johnny in our J3 taildragger, I assumed we were heading out for more in-flight training. Instead, after making a few 'touch n' goes', he directed me to make a full stop landing, then climbed out. Instructors know when their students are ready, but it is a scary moment when heading into the wild blue yonder, on your own.

On takeoff and gaining enough altitude to begin a left turn, the altimeter plummeted to zero. With a large lump in my throat, and squeamish feeling in the pit of my stomach, thankful it wasn't the airspeed indicator that failed, I remembered my instructor's lectures: *'don't depend entirely on your instruments', 'know the attitude of the plane', 'compare its nose to the horizon', 'listen to the sound of your machine!'* Becoming so busy thinking about all that and concentrating on what to do next, I forgot about being up there alone and found myself descending at the end of the runway.

Getting lower and slower, I kept an eye on the airspeed, briefly considering a go-around, but instead, pulled the throttle all the way back and amazingly executed a perfect landing. That was exhilarating! So, I taxied back to the end of the runway and did it again, several times! The excitement felt the same as when learning to ride a bike and 'let go' for the first time; or when the Drivers Ed teacher sends you around the block by yourself…only, magnified!

After attending ground school, I squeezed by with a passing grade on the written exam, accumulated forty hours of solo flight time through cross-country trips, practicing chandelles, figure eights and recovering from high altitude self-induced stalls. With all requirements met, Johnny signed me off for the infamous FAA check ride.

Last minute tips from Instructor Johnny Johnstone
before solo flight in Comanche

Additional hours were racked up in our Cessna 140 and low-wing Comanche, to build hours, and courage, before scheduling an appointment with the intimidating government boys; however, I never got around to taking that final step. Working full-time at Fort Meade Veterans Hospital, and managing a family took precedence over acquiring the status of 'private pilot.' My student permit was sufficient. I was satisfied with reaching my goal and comfortable with accomplishing my main objective.

Texas native, friend and local country music entertainer, Coke Chapman was hired as our fulltime pilot. As Roger's right-hand man he assisted with all facets of our aviation business. Coke was employed at Hamilton Cattle Company near Hayes, SD before he, wife Bonnie and children, Donna Rae and Danny, relocated to the Black Hills. Formerly, they were residents of Faith, South Dakota; a small town located 100 miles east, home of the renowned annual Faith Stock Show, and Roger's birthplace.

Coke Servicing Ag Wagon Spray Plane, Bear Butte in Background

The Chapmans became good friends. We had great times enjoying cookouts, gatherings in our homes, and socializing with mutual friends, usually where Coke's band played which always included the annual Faith Stock Show weekend. This forever-popular historical affair, first organized in 1910, includes street dances, rodeos, carnival rides, barbecues, and amusing competitions such as the '*anything goes*' donkey races!

Unknown donkey puller, Earl Ferguson, Carv Thompson, Roger

The celebration winds down with an outdoor concert featuring top-notch, well-known entertainers. We had the honor of chartering Gunsmoke's Ken Curtis from Rapid City Regional Airport to Faith when he was the featured performer. During the short flight, he and Roger talked and joked in the front. When addressing the kids and me in the back seats, *'Festus'* emerged… proof, that he was indeed the real deal! He was fun-loving, likeable, comical and had a fantastic singing voice. His show was our all-time favorite.

CHAPTER 2

Expansion

New Aircraft Maintenance Shop. Major and minor repair on all types of aircraft.

Charter Service - FAA Approved Flight School.

Cessna Ag Wagon - Sales and Service - Aerial Crop Spraying and Seeding.

First, a large 40 x 50-foot maintenance shop, with ceiling and flooring radiant heat; and two separate hangars were constructed to the east. Then, the terminal building consisting of two restrooms, lounge, and offices were attached to the west side of the shop. The desk in the main office displayed a nameplate reading Hlavka Aviation, Roger Hlavka President. The walls of his office hosted Cessna and Bellanca aircraft glossies, and membership plaques from Sturgis Chamber of Commerce, SD Meat Promoters, SD Stockgrowers, Alkali 4-H Club, Elks Club, Naja Shriners and Pilots International.

A large bulletin board next to the counter displayed a menagerie of shirt tail snippets belonging to many brave student pilots, who had successfully survived their first solo flight. On the desk behind the reception counter, was a similar nameplate, *Jean Hlavka, Office Manager*. There, I had access to the radio base station, intercom, computer, adding machine, typewriter, file cabinet and aviation-related sales items. The large aeronautical map of the United States covering most of the south wall of the lobby, determined mileage from Sturgis to any destination desired. Other walls behind the counter displayed plaques, certificates, and required licenses. Brightly colored commercial carpeting and coordinated seating unit provided comfortable lounging, giving view to fuel pumps, the runway, and historical Bear Butte Mountain to the north. The new modern facility was an attractive, functional, much-needed improvement.

Jean Hlavka, Ofc Manager

Roger Hlavka, President

On standby to assist with our expanding business were four commercial aviators: Dwayne Vig, Faith area rancher/United Airlines captain; Mick Quaal (*Quall*) Perkins County rancher/Vietnam Veteran; John Chamberlain, USAF retiree; and Dick Lemm, pilot at Father Murray's Home for Boys. The experienced pilots, with commitments of their own, made themselves available for charter flights when needed, and were vital in the success that Hlavka Aviation achieved. Our other employee was part-time high school student, Delbert Loughlin; a nice young man, pleasant to be around and brother-in-law to mechanic Jerry. He assisted in the shop, helped with cleanup, planting trees, and with whatever else needed done. He was with us until completing high school, then enlisted in the Marines.

Student pilots often accompanied Roger on charters to gain experience and earn hours. Joining him on a scheduled flight to New Mexico would be brother-in-law, Dewey Rathke. He and Carol, Roger's sister, lived on the Strong-Lloyd Ranch where Dewey began working part-time at age twelve, & later became foreman. The Rathkes formed a partnership with Buster Strong, were co-owners of the ranch located 15 miles east of the Airport. They had their hands full with their operation, raising five daughters, at times a nephew, attending school activities, and serving as 4-H leaders. It was within the past year that Dewey had found time to aggressively pursue his avid interest in flying. He purchased a new Citabria airplane; by checking cattle and accompanying Roger on charter flights, had acquired 100 hours of flight time.

The most adventurous trip the brothers-in-law shared was to Westport, Washington where they participated in a Fishing Derby of 2,000 competitors. From the two plane loads of local businessmen; Dewey pulled in a trophy fish, a twenty-one-pound king salmon.

William J. Brown, Roger, Joe Martin, Dewey

Al Reeder, Coke, Russ Molstad, Gunner Earley, John Eddy

CHAPTER 3

The Day

October 28, 1974, began as usual. Roger was at his office before the rest of us were awake, in preparation for his scheduled charter. He had conducted the pre-flight on our recently purchased twin-engine Beechcraft Baron, filed the required Flight Plan, made business calls and was waiting for his co-pilot to arrive.

Daughter, Lorie Dawn had risen early, a commendable trait her father instilled; son Edward Earl and I were neither as fortunate; but, as always by 7:15 the kids were on time to board their early morning school bus. Only fifteen-months apart, our children were often mistaken for twins, especially in their stocking caps which the brisk autumn morning warranted.

They loved living next to the airport in their new home. Eddie, in his red and blue airplane-bordered room spent time sketching, watching ants farm, combating GI Joes, sorting his Hot Wheels Matchbox collection, operating toy trucks and his mechanical crane. His greatest passion was sculpting clay figures of people, animals, and of course, airplanes. At age nine, his teacher entered him in a statewide art contest, in which he was chosen as one of three outstanding Young Artists in SD; whose works toured libraries, galleries, and schools throughout the state. His fierce twelve inch, fighting pirate did not survive the battle. Unfortunately, when returned it no longer resembled the intricately designed sculpture created; but had transformed into the large clump of artist wax from whence it came.

Lorie, in her upstairs, neighboring pink and white flowery decorated room, could be found stretched out on her canopy bed, reading, listening to her mother's Elvis records, doing homework, creating stories, practicing guitar, or playing Barbies. She had assumed the 'big sister protector role' which her brother tolerated; but, as he grew older, was resenting *'being bossed around'*. They got along quite well, readily standing by each other when the chips were down. They shared other loves: snuggling with their father on thick red shag while watching Andy of Mayberry, two sets of adored grandparents; and our fifth family member, a black lab named Boo!

Lorie and Ed, first on their school bus, always chose to sit together directly behind their favorite driver and friend, Ernie Miller. He and his brother Eddie safely transported countless students, and their parents to music contests and sporting events across the state and beyond.

I blew the kids a series of two-handed kisses, they flashed back their beautiful, spacious smiles and the bus continued east on its circular route. Within the hour, it would fill with farm kids, connect with I-90 at Pleasant Valley, and deliver students to each of the Sturgis schools.

As Boo and I resumed our short walk to the terminal, I felt blest never having to ride a school bus. Equally so, 'going to work' no longer entailed warming the car, scraping ice-covered windshields, and driving a few miles to Fort Meade; simply meant taking a few long strides out my back door. I completed the usual housekeeping chores of straightening the lobby, cleaning bathrooms, emptying trash, vacuuming, filling the pop machine, and making coffee; then went about my routine office duties.

In anticipation of his long-distance run, Dewey had completed his chores earlier than usual. Determined not to be late, he arrived at the airport ahead of schedule to avoid a razzing from his brother-in-law. It didn't work! Roger couldn't help himself, *"Good afternoon Rathke what's the holdup?"*

"Hlavka, you"… Dewey began with his comeback; but was abruptly cut off by the laughter of his sparring partner.

"C'mon Rathke, let's get this bird in the air!" He tossed a quick wink my way, with his 'make you feel good toothy smile'. *"See you later, be back around four o'clock."* I bid the pilots a safe trip as they exited the terminal, stepped onto the tarmac, and boarded the Baron at 9:30 am, the exact time planned for takeoff.

Roger's teeth, slightly protuberant, often brought about comments due to their natural whiteness. *'Never drank a glass of milk, had a cavity or been to a dentist'*, was always his quick response. From the time we married, I hadn't known him to see a dentist or medical doctor, except for his required annual pilot's physical. When employed at Wood and Kullbom Dental Clinic as receptionist and 'fill-in' dental assistant, I convinced Roger to have his bothersome wisdom teeth checked. Oral surgeon, Dr. Terrance Kullbom advised two visits to have them extracted. However, due to Roger's busy schedule, insistence and impatience; Terry hesitantly agreed to remove all four impactions during one visit.

Following the procedure, Roger was to go home, take a pain pill, lie down flat, and stay there for the rest of the day. Under no circumstance was he to fly! These strict instructions, written in bold red letters across Roger's dental records were, of course, ignored. He returned directly to the airport and gave lessons throughout the afternoon.

All was well until the middle of the night, when discovering Roger's blood-soaked pillow. I called Terry and was instructed to get him to the clinic immediately, where he received a mouth full of cotton balls, gauze, an injection to relax him *and*; a well-deserved lecture on the importance of following doctors' orders. He spent the rest of the night lying flat in a dental chair, with a needle stuck in his arm. After several days when the swelling went down and was able to chew, Roger gave his doctor a call, apologized for being 'a little rough on him' and invited the Kullboms to join us for dinner and a night on the town.

While watching Roger and Dewey taxi onto the runway, lift off and head south on their flight to New Mexico, my mind was on the Weyers (*Wires*) and what they must be going through while anticipating the arrival of three deceased family members. Squelch on the two-way radio interrupted my thoughts. I acknowledged an incoming plane, gave the pilot clearance to land, and returned to my desk to tackle mounting paperwork.

It had been a little over one year, since leaving my job as ward secretary at Fort Meade Veterans Hospital, to assist full-time with the increasing demands of our business. I enjoyed being my own boss, meeting interesting travelers, working with the public, and being part of all the action that took place at the busy airport which became very active during the world-famous Sturgis Motorcycle Rally.

Students practiced touch n' goes, planes refueled. Pilot friends from town dropped by for rolls and coffee, and as always; stood at the counter played several hands of pitch at quarter a game--quarter a set, talked shop with the mechanics, and discussed our upcoming Fly-in Appreciation Days.

As secretary/treasurer of South Dakota Aviation Trades Association, I worked on the program, recruited speakers, and scheduled entertainment for the annual convention to be held in December at the Ramada in Rapid City, and confirmed our flight to DC for the National Ag Aviation Trades Conference in January. Roger, as president of SDATA was on the national board, and required to attend both events. We were looking forward to another trip to the east coast, this time with the kids joining us.

First Trip Capitol Bldg., DC with SD Rep, Jim Abnor

CHAPTER 4

The Call

Roger and Dewey had not yet returned by four o'clock; nor had I received notification of the delay. At 4:15, Boo & I left to greet the kids. He deposited himself by the roadside facing west, wagging eagerly while waiting for his bosom buddies. Inside, I flipped on the lights, checked on supper stewing in the crockpot, and cranked up the heat. As the first ones to be dropped off the busload of rambunctious students, daylight would provide the kids time to burn off steam riding bikes, play on their large schoolyard-type swing set, constructed by Roger and crew; and as always, check-in at the office, where leftover rolls might still be available for their consumption.

I sat at the dining room table with a fresh cup of coffee, enjoying the picturesque view of the Black Hills to the west, while watching for the bus when the phone rang... *"Hlavka Aviation, this is Jean."*

"Ma'am, this is Flight Service, Rapid City Airport. Has twin engine 414K landed at Sturgis Airport? They have not extended or closed their flight plan; we are unable to make contact with the aircraft!"

With tightly squeezed eyes and clenched teeth, I sucked in a shallow breath and held it. A wave of numbness and paralyzing silence overtook me. It must have been mere seconds, but seemed an eternity before hearing a faint, distant, *"Ma'am, Ma'am, are you ok, are you there... Ma'am?"*

I retrieved the dangling phone from the wall before me, pressed it hard against my stomach and held it there momentarily...*"Sir, I think I heard what you said, but would you please repeat!"* There was composed urgency in the young man's voice when responding politely in a deliberate methodical manner. He repeated word for word, what I had clearly heard the first time!

Hoping beyond hope, I slid open the dining room door, praying the twin would be making its approach, or I would hear its overhead engine. But that was not to be. *"Negative sir, the aircraft has not yet arrived! What do we do now??"*

"Stay calm", was the controller's first instruction. Then he requested I contact Flight Control immediately if hearing from the pilot, or if the aircraft lands. He informed me that all surrounding airports had been contacted and if nothing developed within one half hour a Missing Aircraft Alert would be filed, and an extensive six-state air search would begin. *"We'll keep in touch,"* he assured, *"and will notify you of any developments."* It felt as if my head would explode from swirling thoughts: *stay calm, stay calm...he says! I'm trying! Why no radio contact... ELT signal, a distress call? Roger would have turned around if in trouble... contacted the tower... somebody! Why didn't he?*

I kept reassuring myself that there was some logical reason, an explanation! There had to be! Their trip had taken them close to the border; perhaps forced into Mexico? Hijacked? They could have been, it was happening, there had been reports!

Feeling light-headed and dizzy, I tried to shake off everything going through my head; I could barely think, let alone talk; but had to! Marty and the Weyer family were waiting. Marty and I had known each other since eighth grade, graduated high school together. After college, he and brother Clint attended mortuary school, and had taken over Jolley Funeral Home, previously operated by their father and grandfather before them.

Marty, as an amateur pilot and member of the Bear Butte Flying Club, was a regular at the airport. I needed to call my good friend but hesitated; hoping at any moment the phone would ring, that Roger or Flight Service would put an end to this nightmarish experience! I couldn't hold off any longer and pleaded with God to give me the strength to do what had to be done...*"Marty, this is Jean."*

"Hi there, been expecting your call, I'll be..." he began, but I interrupted.

"Marty... Roger isn't here. I don't know when... or if he ever will be? Flight Service called; he hasn't closed his flight plan." Not wanting to lose control, I tried to slow down, took a deep breath, but it was extremely difficult to stay calm. I didn't know if my continual rambling even made sense...*nothing* was making any sense!! It all seemed surreal, like it wasn't really happening! *"They're unable to make contact with him. They're starting a search. I don't know what to do! What about the Weyer family? They've been through so much already. Marty, what do I do? I can't handle this!"*

He responded calmly with sensitive reassuring confidence, *"Jean, it's ok, you're ok. I'll take care of it."* I knew he could. Marty was in the business of handling difficult situations, of showing compassion to others; but more importantly, he was naturally one of the nicest guys around. In high school, he was our Senior Class President, chosen not only due to his leadership skills; he was well-liked, everybody's friend.

Languishing over what to do next, I tried to decide what was best! Do I tell the kids? Call my parents? Roger's parents? No, I wouldn't say anything to them or the kids, not yet. I couldn't allow them to know the fear I felt or think the thoughts I had.... that Roger and Dewey could be lying somewhere hurt, needing help? I became physically sickened thinking about the worse scenario; that seven children could be fatherless. No, I would wait; surely someone, anyone, would call with an explanation that everything was all right, that it was some huge, terrible mistake. I wouldn't say anything, not now, except to my sister-in- law, but dreaded having to make the call.

In my entire life had I ever had to do anything more difficult, than when reaching for the phone to call Carol! It was well past the time the guys were due back, and knew she'd be checking on them at any moment. Still hoping and praying *someone* would call with good news, after a series of extended breaths pulled from the deepest depths of my gut, I dialed the phone. When she answered, I paused briefly, to swallow, hoping that would help conceal my anguish... *"Carol,* I opened my mouth to continue...nothing came out except a shaky sigh.

"Jean? Are you ok?" Hearing her voice was comforting, the tension throughout my body relaxed some.

"No…not really! I'm concerned that Roger and Dewey aren't back." I tried to ease into the call received. She responded calmly as we exchanged reasons and excuses for their delay. We both knew they would have notified Flight Control of any change of plans or transmitted an emergency alert if in trouble! Why hadn't they? Where *were* they! Somebody somewhere must have seen or heard something! They couldn't have just evaporated into thin air - but it seemed they had!

Carol is a private person, caring and strong. Unlike her brother, kept thoughts to herself, didn't speak her mind or reveal emotions easily. We discussed other things, but mostly about our greatest concern: her five daughters, ages six to fourteen; and my son and daughter, ages ten and eleven. We talked about what to do next, about what could have gone wrong! Surely, there was something we hadn't thought of, but what!

Could they have stopped to see a friend, relative; someone they knew along the way? Had engine trouble, radio failure? Hijacked? Perhaps some physical ailment arose, that needed treatment? Between the two of us, we had exhausted our brains; thought of every situation that could have prevented them from contacting us; which included the worst possibility; but didn't go there. At this point, we agreed there wasn't much that *could* be done… except wait!

CHAPTER 5

The Night

It was a clear, calm chilly night with Boo at my side as I waited, watched, and paced back and forth from the deck through the sliding glass door to the kitchen. Boo had taken on the role as my self-appointed guardian. Each time when going inside, he waited by the door for my return, then greeted me as though I'd been gone for days. When I sat, he sat beside me, cocked his head, and whined. When I pet him and slid my hand along his silky black coat, he reciprocated by placing his soft paw on my knee, as if to say, *'somethings wrong, I'm here for you'.*

Forcing myself to concentrate on positive things, I focused on the old wooden shed and thought of my friend, Judy Walker. We and other students spent hours there, helping each other prepare for the written pilot's exam. Our first office and makeshift lounge, now vacated, was being used only for storage; but served as a reminder of what came from that rickety old building, and how far things had progressed!

The autumn sky was bright, lit up by masses of twinkling stars. Scanning the unending wonderment, I looked for designs and formations that could be made out to be something; a house, an animal, faces…like as a kid, and finding all sorts of shapes when staring wide-eyed into infinity. Assuming the larger lights with a steady beam were planets, I attempted to name them, but my count was always off; wasn't sure of Pluto's status and kept forgetting the one that had just turned upside down and inside out!

It is amazing what your imagination does, when running rampant! Sometimes, when focused intently on stars some appeared to move and make slightly audible sounds, such as the hum of a distant plane, but never grew louder, nor came closer. Once, I discovered faint lights alternating from green to red. They were far away and moved, but very slowly.

It was a plane, the first seen; but too high and came from the north. Roger would be lower, coming from the south. The blinking lights continued in a distant southerly path, diminishing until no longer visible. Guessing it was either a military plane heading to Ellsworth Air Force Base, or an airliner scheduled to land at Rapid City Airport, I stepped inside, filled a coffee mug, and returned to the deck with a warm blanket large enough for two.

Except for my pacing, and Boo following my every step the only other movement throughout that unnerving night was a repetitive rotating beacon. Again and again, it made rounds, casting a bluish hue upon metal hangars, the tie-down area, past the terminal, and northwest onto the runway. It scanned westward, lighting the old building and shelterbelt behind, flashed south across the deck and the sliding glass door, then illuminated the parking lot to the east, and steadily continued, over and over on its' endless path. It was comforting when reaching the house, like a predictable, steadfast friend… the same as the one beside me. I was thankful for him and that beacon watching over us.

When talking to Boo, he seemed to understand. His soft, compassionate eyes eased my helpless feeling. I told him about his distant cousin Joe, who was also deeply loved. *"He looked like you, was my protector, crazy about water, and very smart … the same as you,"*! I shared an encounter Joe had with a porcupine, tapped Boo's shiny nose, and warned, *"don't go poking this where it doesn't belong, it's very painful to have quills removed. Something else you should know…just because you're a professional swimmer, doesn't mean, you can't drown"*; then shared a time when Joe almost met his 'waterloo'!

My brothers and I, with Joe ever-present, spent a lot of time at the Cheyenne River five-span railroad bridge just east of our home near Wasta, South Dakota. The fear of God put into us by our parents, kept us out of deep water and off ice. The only thing we knew about swimming, we learned from Joe, in Dog Paddling 101, although it was difficult to test our abilities in ankle-deep water. Most of the river had frozen over when Joe was fetching twigs, happily slipping, and sliding! He was several feet out, near the open channel when breaking through thin ice. Disoriented, he frantically swam in circles beneath the ice, striking upward with his strong head, trying desperately to get air into his nostrils while searching for an escape.

We stood on the bank, hollering, crying, and calling him while throwing rocks into the hole, hoping to help Joe locate his only possibility of getting out. Eventually he came closer and closer to his point of entry and sole exit. We made even more noise yelling, encouraging, and praising him when his shiny black nose poked up. He pawed at crumbling ice, with sharp claws gripping the slippery surface he worked his way toward us. Perhaps by then his back feet could push against the bottom. Somehow, after several attempts, he was able to free himself from his trip to hell.

He could barely shake himself off, but continually wagged his strong black rudder as if to show us what kept him from meeting his demise. When we hugged him, kissed him, and rubbed his soggy coat he licked our faces. Usually, we turned down his slobbers; this time, we didn't. That was a good lesson, we stopped playing Fetch on ice; but Joe taught us the value of persistence… to never give up!

During story time, Boo cocked his head with perked ears. He listened intently, the same as a child when hearing the story 'The Three Bears' and learning that entering strange, unfamiliar places can be dangerous. When concluding my account of Joe's *death-defying* adventure, Boo's big brown eyes rolled upward, locked with mine and cocked his head, as if he 'got it'. Both he and Joe were very close to being human! They took on a different form, spoke another language, but were amazing communicators!

When returning from my brief reprieve, fear and worry once again enveloped me, and my pacing resumed. That was disturbing. It reminded me of times when witnessing that excessive behavior; but now, found myself doing the same!

Every morning at 7:15 five days a week when aides permitted my entrance through the heavy steel door and into the locked ward at Fort Meade Veterans Hospital, an elderly catatonic gentleman awaited my arrival. His forehead revealed evidence of having received a lobotomy after his violent tendencies manifested, either during or following World War II. Always, when politely acknowledging his presence with a smile and friendly greeting, he remained silent, expressionless, and simply resumed his incessant pacing.

With hands clasped behind his back and head bowed, he traipsed back and forth from the south end of the long hallway and past my office to the entrance door repeatedly. On one occasion, without warning he lunged through the open door of my office. He slid across the desk, knocking to the floor my typewriter, a pile of papers *and,* the doctor who only moments before had been standing beside me; but now, suddenly found himself down, with angry hands gripped around his throat.

It took two strong male aides to remove the captor from atop his prey, whose bizarre behavior often gave staff reason to believe he could easily be one of the patients. My buddy must have thought I was being threatened, or it was just a great opportunity to get even! He vehemently disliked the doctor for mocking and humiliating him in group sessions; and ordering his electroshock treatments. I was fine, the doctor was fine; however, the patient was not as fortunate. He received solitary confinement and increased ECT. Due to the emergence of effective psychiatric medication, that procedure is in decline and controversial; but still used for severe depression, mania, and schizophrenia. It is not pleasant to watch!

The other time when observing extreme pacing was at the Hill City Zoo. That was always one of the stops when touring the southern Black Hills with our parents. At the entrance was a cage too small for the large grey wolf confined there. The once proud, beautiful animal was oblivious to gawking tourists as he paced along the dirt path that big paws had tamped into a deep rut. That saddened me, wanted him to be free, roaming the wilderness to the east in high mountaintops with tall evergreen trees and freshwater creeks; the place from which familiar callings came, the place where he belonged! The last time we were there, he was gone. I chose to believe the howls echoing through rugged, rocky canyons were happy sounds... his!

Pacing is a normal coping tool. At least I convinced myself of that, because that is what I continued to do and considered myself to be somewhat normal! I decided both humans *and* animals resort to pacing when in situations they cannot change; or don't know what else to do, when experiencing hopelessness.

When attempting to concentrate on good times, happy memories; my mind was preoccupied; stuck in survival mode. I thought of all the different possibilities that Roger and Dewey could be facing if finding themselves in a hopeless, desperate life-or-death situation, and considered all the 'what-ifs'; stories I'd heard of people in dire situations, who had beaten all odds! Roger and Dewey would fall into that category. They were strong men, resourceful, and would do whatever was humanly possible to save themselves!

One of my father's stories came to mind from his library of many 'life's true tales' that he shared with his children and grandchildren, when pressed to do so. His survival story was similar to Joe's.

Dad had a close relationship with relatives, especially his double cousins. Their mothers, Ethel and Mary Harwood were sisters, their fathers, Wesley and Walter Ferguson, brothers. Always together, he and his cousins were more like siblings. As teenagers, when riding herd on range cattle and allowing the horses to drink at a deep dugout, they decided to swim across. Not knowing how, dad put his arms around the shoulders of the other two and paddled his legs.

Halfway out, weighed down, tiring from being pushed under; the swimmers released him and headed to shore. Left in the deep hole of water, thrashing and gulping for air dad immediately sank down into muck below. When bending his knees, squatting forward and giving a hard push, he was able to free his mud- stuck feet. By cupping hands and pulling strong arms downward, he could make it to the top. With lungs ready to burst and gasping for air, he went down again. On his third attempt to get closer to shore he felt someone grab his hair, drag him through a slimy, mossy film, and throw him over a large sharp rock. Water gushed from his limp body as his cousins shook him until he started coughing, vomiting, then breathing. He was forever grateful to his cousin George, the one who after catching his breath; swam back out and saved my father's life!

But that was then, another time, another place; now, it was Boo and me attempting to comfort each other on a lonely deck cooling in the night air. His large furry frame was not enough to completely ward off the chill. I gently lifted his head from my lap to retrieve a warm jacket. When promising him, "I'll be back", a surge of panic circuited through me, which to that point, had been somewhat successfully contained! Roger had said that when he and Dewey left the day before. He always did when leaving, usually with a two-fingered flip of the wrist, a wink and his broad smile!

This wasn't like Roger to be late! That's how it is, in the aviation business. Pilots try to be on, or ahead of their ETA. If not, they always notify Flight Service to prevent panic. Roger had experienced panic once, when sleeping! I hadn't given that ordeal much thought until now, when everything imaginable was racing through my head.

It was in the middle of the night, just a few months back when Roger abruptly sat up in bed, sweating profusely; repeating, *"What the hell! What the hell?"*

My mood, always on the grumpy side when disturbed from deep sleep, in my groggy agitated state I groaned, *"What on earth are you doing? You scared the life out of me!"*

He blew out a lengthy sigh of relief, *"Scared… Scared? You should have been, where I've been!"* With a string of strong expletives, he got up and turned on the blinding overhead light, *"I couldn't get away, couldn't get out!"* While wiping away beads of sweat from his face with both hands; he hesitated, calmed down a bit, then described his frightful encounter.

"I was trapped in a large, dark attic-like room with an ugly, evil-looking woman, chasing and stabbing at me with a long-bladed knife. There were no windows, doors or openings of any kind! I was trying my damndest…but couldn't escape." He breathed deeply, then continued in his typical fast-talking manner, *"Guess it was some sort of weird nightmare, or premonition! Don't know, but it scared the hell out of me!"* Then, Roger made a joke that made me laugh and agree with him…. something about changing his ways! He showered, dressed, and left

for the office. I rolled over, went back to sleep, and the 'whatever' was never talked about again.

Those experiences that my father and Roger shared were generations apart, different but same; the same helplessness that Joe faced, the same as I now felt; defenseless, vulnerable. The only other time in my entire life, when feeling such emotion was not life-threatening; but made me fearful, very sad and alone!

I was a shy five-year-old in first grade at Wasta, SD. Our teacher was a stern elderly lady with snowy white hair, who should have retired years ago. We beginners sat in little red wooden chairs with twisted crosswires tightly stretched to legs below. Mother had dressed me in a long-sleeved silk blouse, grey wool skirt with suspenders, long brown cotton leggings attached to a garter belt and black patent leather shoes, with buckles. As a wiggler, I had entangled my feet beneath the chair where buckles became hung up on the taut wire. Attempts to free myself had failed. At recess, the teacher dismissed us. The others were rapidly leaving the classroom when she approached, wanting to know what was wrong with me. Embarrassed about the predicament I had gotten myself into, I remained silent. *"Well, young lady"* she gruffed, *"you don't want to go outside with the other children?"*

"Uh-huh," I replied while nodding meekly *...but I'm stuck."* Her next comments caused me to have feelings of intense dislike, never known before. That's when promising myself, if ever becoming a teacher, would never be a mean one like her; but like my mama, a good teacher, kind and who at that moment, was needed badly!

"Well," she repeated sarcastically, *"you got yourself into this situation. If you can't get out, just stay there!"* I vividly remember how awful I felt; ashamed, imprisoned by a chair, abandoned by my teacher. I couldn't see where she went…...long thick hair and cupped

hands were covering my face, hiding tears. I thought she might have gone to the playground to prevent the others from having fun, or maybe not; she could be at her desk, watching me, waiting. It was very difficult not to squirm, but didn't dare. Afraid to move at all or ask permission to use the bathroom; I did what she had warned, *"Sit there, and be still!"*

When recess was over, my older brother came to me wanting to know what was wrong, then freed me from my humiliation. After we arrived home from school, Dale told our parents what had happened. Dad, as Chairman of the School Board immediately called a special emergency meeting, that evening!! He had experienced somewhat the same as I had. As a first grader was grabbed by his male teacher, shook for *'not paying attention'* and slammed back into his desk. This caused the buttons on his brand-new white shirt, sewn by his mama, to pop off! That was the most upsetting for him; for me, I didn't understand why my teacher was punishing, instead of helping me.

The next day when arriving at school, a nice, friendly lady greeted us. It wasn't just because of what happened to me that caused the magical disappearance of our grumpy teacher; she did other despicable things, like making a student eat a whole jar of white paste, just because he tasted it!

After hearing so many stories about school from his older siblings, our little brother decided he wasn't going to that awful place. When forced to do so, he developed a plan. The first day of school and several occasions after that, he ran home. Regardless of how long they stayed, when my parents left, he was out of there! Eventually, he realized school wasn't really the bad place he had been led to believe; earned a college degree and had a successful career as a high school teacher and girls' basketball coach at Marshalltown, Iowa.

That is how the first night was spent; thinking about the past, afraid of the future, talking to 'a dog', drinking coffee, and waiting…. waiting for the sound of an airplane engine or for the phone to ring. Except for a few calls back and forth with Carol, encouraging each other with attempts to subdue emerging panic, the phone remained silent.

When the comforting repetitive light dimmed, a glow to the east increased, flickering stars faded and sky lightened; I felt relief. Finally, the horrible night was ending; and two unsuspecting children would be waking. Little did I know that it was only an introduction, a sneak preview into many never-ending days and long, agonizing sleepless nights to come.

CHAPTER 6

The Unknown/Strange Happenings

The kids came into the kitchen early, questioning the absence of their father. Not wanting to frighten them, I simply explained he hadn't made it home yet, and tried to assure them that everything would be all right, but how? How do you prepare children for the unknown?

I urged them to finish the oatmeal they were dabbling in, and get ready for the bus; then phoned my parents, not knowing what to say, or how? I managed a feeble... *"Dad?"*

The uncertainty in my voice, and the fact that I hadn't ever called them so early in the morning, alerted him, *"Honey, what's wrong?"*

I tried to maintain composure, enough to cover up the fright that had invaded me, but the *'honey'* stirred a little girl inside, whom he had comforted many times! Between sniffs and quivering breaths, I explained the same thing to him as I had to the kids: 'we didn't know what was going on, Roger was missing, he hadn't made it home, and didn't know why!' I told him about the all-out air search that had been put in place. To protect them from all sorts of stories that no doubt would be floating around, we decided the kids shouldn't attend school, Dad would come get them. They were excited about getting to play hooky -- better yet, to be spending the night in the arms of their loving grandparents.

The next morning when arriving at the office the guys were already aware of something seriously wrong when neither the Baron, nor Roger were there. He was always in his office early, long before anyone else. I shared information received the night before; that search plans were being initiated by the local CAP, as well as Four Corners Search and Rescue Headquarters at Pagosa Springs, Colorado.

The first telephone call came from KBHB, the local radio station that had received word of the search and wanting information; then, calls came from KOTA TV, Rapid City Journal, and the Sturgis Tribune. From that point on, the telephone rang nonstop from friends, acquaintances, even total strangers offering help with whatever was needed. After work, I went to be with the kids, to tell them how much their father loved them and that everything would be fine but couldn't convince them.

Upon seeing the eagerness in their big brown bewildered eyes, I wanted to tell them more – something, anything to make them feel better, but how? How do you explain the inexplicable, when there are no answers, only questions? How do you protect children from insensitive comments and speculations?

"We don't know what is going on", I confessed; *"but we need to be brave and try to stay strong for each other."* Then, told them about all the calls we were receiving from friends, neighbors, and strangers who were concerned about us, their father, Uncle Dewey, Aunt Carol, and their cousins. The kids agreed to stay with their grandma for a few more days. I explained my need to be near the phone, *"I love you always and forever, and promise you will be the first to know when I hear anything"*.

Upon leaving, I shared a pre-arranged plan, *"Oh, I almost forgot,"* I quipped, *"you and Grandma can decide whether you go to school, or not; that's up to you and her."* That brought about two wide grins that warmed my heart, *"You guys are so cute when you smile."* Dad came home with me that night and spent the next several days helping out and appeasing Boo, who was noticeably feeling abandoned.

From the day the quest began to locate our husbands and Weyer family members, the children were keenly aware of their mothers' involvement in the search. With God's help, family, caring friends, and overwhelming community support, Carol and I reached out to anyone we thought could help. We continually and aggressively pursued all possibilities, suggestions and recommendations; while making a conscious effort to conceal our frustration and disappointment from the kids, when futile attempts and false leads went nowhere.

Retaining the slightest degree of normalcy in our children's daily lives was an impossibility, as was protecting them from the cruel world of reality. They should have been doing what kids do best; having fun, goofing off and enjoying a stable, carefree childhood. Instead, they were burdened with uncertainty, confusion, and fear. It was extremely painful to witness their anguish as they yearned for their fathers, and worried for their mothers' safety, as we dealt with the challenges and daunting tasks the ironic situation presented.

I kept track of all information, particularly for the children when they were older, when they might have unresolved questions. Moreso, they needed to know about the magnitude of concern and effort put forth by so many who cared about them, as they suffered through the unaccountable disappearance of their fathers. Every phone call placed and received was noted, as well as names, contacts, addresses, ideas, suggestions, and thoughts. All correspondence, newspaper articles, documents, and investigative reports were saved for when someday, a complete accounting of the search could be available for them, if ever wanting to know more.

During the day, I attempted to complete office work between continual calls and offers of help; other times, stayed busy repeating housekeeping and menial tasks to keep from thinking. Days intermingled with nights which were often spent at the office doing bookwork. After going home, I researched my bible, read favorite passages and scripture; until tired enough to sleep. Psalm 46:1-3 described our situation best.

(soft instrumental 'Amazing Grace' in background)

'God is our refuge and strength, an ever-present
help in times of trouble.

*Therefore, we will not fear, though the earth
gives way, and the mountains fall into the heart of
the sea, when waters roam and foam, and mountains
quake with their surging'.*

I began losing weight, couldn't sleep, wasn't hungry, couldn't eat; Roger and Dewey could be down in the mountains or captive somewhere, cold and starving! The range of emotional fluctuations was indescribable: disbelief, despair…then hope; betrayal, abandonment…then guilt; compassion…then self- pity; but always feeling emptiness, sometimes anger, or perhaps that was deep frustration felt when not understanding why God was taking so long, why Roger hadn't been more careful!! Our questions needed answers, but there were none, only opinions, thoughts, theories. Many felt they had been hijacked, forced to fly into Mexico. A local psychic insisted we concentrate on Wyoming. Our insurance agent approached me, advising I prepare for a liability suit!

Strange Happenings~

Strange occurrences began within the first week of Roger's disappearance. After working late into the night, arriving home, checking on the kids sleeping soundly and dimming the lights; I flopped into a lounger in our downstairs rec room. Not yet asleep or totally awake; was in a deeply relaxed state when something startled me! When leaning forward and looking upward… it was Roger! He was vaguely draped in something light blue, the same color as his eyes. I began rapidly firing questions!

"Where in the world, are you!! Why were you gone so long? How could you do this to us!" He remained silent and while looking down peacefully, smiled. When reaching toward him, he retracted, did not communicate verbally; just continued to show his wide trademark. There was a complete calmness about him which was quite unusual. Roger rarely relaxed.

I tossed out more questions, *"What happened? Are you ok?"* Then he slowly faded away and was gone! Was that an answer, was it really Roger or…. an angel? I didn't know, but whatever it was, it was unexplainable but real. Was he telling me something, something felt, something I knew in my heart: but couldn't share with anyone… that he wasn't coming back? Nobody would believe what I'd experienced, could hardly believe it myself! I hoped for more visits: that he would tell me something, offer more information! There were…but always the same, without answers!

Business, except for the shop, had all but come to a stop. The crew was trying their best to stay focused on work, but none of us were functioning adequately, how could we! The one who put it together and held it there was gone; we were concentrating on our foremost concern… finding him! Coke had been in Colorado since day one of the search. The others, as well as several local pilots, were also making plans to fly to Search Headquarters, except for Ivan. He was our mainstay, our backbone, the wise one -- who everyone went to with any question having to do with airplanes.

Feeling useless, not accomplishing much, I struggled with whether to go or not! What about the kids? I felt guilty leaving them when they needed me most. I didn't want them worrying about me as well; yet I needed to find their father! If I went it had to be now, winter storms would soon put a halt to all ground and air searches in the area where the plane would likely be, if down. I didn't trust flying over the mountains in a small craft. Driving was out of the question. That would take much too long. Roger's brother Bill had come home from Colorado to support his parents, to help with whatever he could and offered to go with me, suggesting the airlines. In the middle of wrestling with my jumbled mind, the phone rang.

"Jean, this is Glen, Glen Best. What can I do to help?" Glen had retired from his lengthy career as Pennington County Sheriff. He and Roger knew each other as neighboring county law enforcement officers and were fellow Shriners. I'd known Glen since his marriage to Betsy Land. She and her family were dear friends and neighbors, when living at Wasta. It was her sister, Joy, who saved my spindly six-year-old body from becoming human dog food! *"I'll take you to Colorado anytime you want to go."* Glen paused, waiting for my reply; but I was busy thanking God for the sudden response to my

dilemma. *"I can be at the Sturgis Airport whenever"*, he continued, *"I have room for two more in my twin, if you have somebody in mind."*

"Thank you, Glen, thank you! I've worked myself into a quandary trying to decide whether to go down there. *You're an answer to prayer! How about tomorrow morning? That will give Roger's brother time; I'm sure he will go with me."*

"Glad to help, I'll be there tomorrow morning as early as you want. Call me back with a time". I thanked Glen again, called my parents to see if they were available to tend the kids; then called my brother-in-law.

CHAPTER 7

Search Headquarters Pagosa Springs Civil Air Patrol

At one point during the short flight, it was as though a powerful magnet had attached itself to my seat and was pulling me downward. I glanced over at Bill seated beside me, *"Did you feel that?"*

He rose with a mysterious look, *"Yah, what the hell?"*

I leaned forward, *"Glen, what was …that?"*

His response was concerning, *"Don't know, what are you talking about?"*

I had been experiencing unexplainable happenings lately and rather than share details, I answered, *"Um, nothing I guess, where are we?"*

Due to the overcast and high altitude of the twin-engine aircraft, Glen could not pinpoint our exact location but informed me that we were above a range of mountains about 14,000 feet, approximately ten miles east of the airport, and would be descending shortly. He picked up the hand mic, identified his aircraft, gave our coordinates, and requested clearance for landing at the Pagosa Springs Airport. *"Be careful,"* the controller warned, *"It's not that great up there, snowstorms forecasted. We're already looking for one in that area."* How well we knew all about the last unnecessary bit of information offered!

Upon landing at search headquarters, Bill and I met with a caravan of friends from home. Keith and Sue Keffler had organized the group to join ground search crews who were being briefed, issued maps, coordinates, and two-way radios. I spent the rest of the day there, then left with Sue to our motel.

That evening we talked about what could be done; about Carol, her five girls, my two children and the Keffeler family. Keith and Sue were both pilots. They and their two children, a boy & girl, lived just east of Sturgis Airport. They were good friends of ours and the Rathkes, the first in the community to help with whatever was needed. Not that they weren't extremely busy with their extensive farm operation; they just always had time for the needs of others.

Early the next morning I woke to the sounds of my own voice, yelling, *"Pull up...pull up! Roger...pull up!"* Sue, awakened by the commotion, was on her feet immediately. In my disoriented frantic half-asleep state, it took a moment or two, before realizing I was safe in a motel room with my friend; not, seconds away from crashing into a mountain. Then I began a runaway, nonstop account of the terrifying experience!

"That was so real, so vivid, it was terrible! Awful! I was there, in the rear of an airplane, leaning forward with my arms placed on the back of the front seats. Roger and Dewey were talking and laughing when I looked out the front of the plane. We were headed straight for a huge snow-covered mountain. I warned them to turn! They ignored me. Louder and louder, I warned them; but they kept talking and joking around, as if I wasn't there. They couldn't hear me, wouldn't listen, wouldn't turn! They didn't see the mountain! I was screaming at Roger to pull up, to do something; when I heard myself yelling!"

That frightening ordeal was totally exhausting! After assuring Sue I wasn't having some sort of nervous breakdown; and without any thought of sleep being an option, we left to join the others for breakfast, filled with uncertainty, not knowing what the day would bring.

The Civil Air Patrol~

Four Corners Civil Patrol had organized an amazing, concentrated search. Pilots had flown in from Utah, New Mexico, Colorado, Arizona, Wyoming, South Dakota, and Nebraska; men and women of all professions with a common goal -- to find fellow pilots. Snowstorms were coming, moving in for the winter. Time was short. I flew with Coke. If the plane was here, we both felt it would be found close to the flight plan route. Focusing on this area, we skimmed mountaintops, scanning crevices and draws. Doubling back, we checked every glint, every shimmering object, and for disturbances in the snow. The mountains were rugged, powerful, and defiant! After a couple of hours of seeing nothing but elk trails and the shadow of our plane, we returned to Pagosa Airport.

The next day I remained there; kept the coffee pot full, served rolls, sandwiches, and cake, helped keep the lounge and bathrooms tidy, introduced myself, thanked pilots, and read incoming reports. It was the sixth day pilots from seven states and NASA had flown one hundred ninety-nine planes, three hundred nineteen sorties, and a total of six hundred ninety hours. Four of those days were concentrated on Blanco Canyon, where three to six feet of snow had accumulated. Fifty-five ground crews, using two hundred twenty-eight vehicles covered 3,614 square miles. The information was astounding, when realizing how much time and effort was put forth, mostly from total strangers. How in the world do you show appreciation for such selfless actions while putting their lives in danger! And to think, most of them would do it all over again, but not tomorrow. The search had been called off, due to the incoming storm.

Early the next morning with Jerry piloting, Dick Lemm and I left Pagosa Springs in the company Cessna. I felt defeated, helpless, frustrated, and an overpowering sense of guilt for leaving. We headed south to skirt around the treacherous, hostile, defiant mountains. As we flew alongside the towering jagged snow- capped peaks, I felt insignificant; the same as when looking out across an endless ocean! Without warning, waves of tearful emotions took over. We were forced to leave, what more could we do, what could anybody do about anything? The future looked very bleak!

It had to be uncomfortable for the guys being subjected to my meltdown. Before long, I got myself under control, apologized to them for having to put up with my mental collapse, and thanked Jerry for looking after me. He was easy-going, a rock, loyal friend, a highly skilled mechanic, and excellent pilot. We were with the Burnhams often. Jerry had perfected barbecued ribs down to a science! His wife Carolyn made fantastic desserts and exceptional candies. They had three children: Cindy the oldest, Scot the youngest and middle child, named Roger.

Upon landing at Sturgis Airport, it felt good to be home with my children. It was encouraging to hear that KBHB and First Western Bank were promoting a Hlavka-Rathke Search Fund. Within two days, the community had contributed several thousand dollars to assist pilots and ground crews with expenses and fuel, their generosity continued. A few weeks later, I received an updated report from Col. Henjum, Air Force Rescue Coordinator. In two separate searches, ***one thousand forty-six personnel*** from seven states used two hundred thirty-eight planes, two hundred thirty-four vehicles, two hundred radios and spent eight hundred thirty-six hours covering 5,054 square miles. There was no way of knowing how many others searched privately.

CHAPTER 8

The Private Investigator Contacts/Correspondence

At the urging of Roger's brother, I contacted Mr. Thomas R. Gutheinz, Checkmate Inc., Lakewood Colorado, member of International Association of Chiefs of Police, International Association for Identification and Evidence, and Photographers International Council. On November 23, 1974, we hired the private investigator who sounded professional and trustworthy. I never met him personally, but pictured him to be 45-50ish, tall, confident, and in good physical shape -- assuming how a man in his profession, would be. He began performing a thorough and extensive investigation on November 25th. On November 27th, his trip to Sturgis revealed no problems with the Hlavka or Rathke families, nor issues with mental or business matters. No foul play was involved in the Sturgis area. Furthermore, he determined that neither Roger nor Dewey would have reason to consummate a disappearance of this magnitude.

Mr. Gutheinz kept in touch with me throughout his investigation, sharing leads, reports, and information. His contacts included those who last spoke with Roger: Atsidi Aviation at the Gallup Airport when adding prop deicer noted both engines were using a lot of oil and added six quarts; Rollie Mortuary employees, who around 3:30 pm delivered the bodies to the airport, and Gallup Municipal FSS with whom no radio contact was received after Roger filed his return flight plan requesting weather conditions at 3:45 pm, and was cautioned by FSS. Roger responded that the twin was not equipped with oxygen; and would go around if the weather deteriorated.

At Gallup, on the 28th it was fair and broken; to the north was marginal with icing conditions at 9,200 feet. Federal Air Regulations, Flight Rule 91.32 states that a civil aircraft may not be operated at 12,500-14,000 altitudes for longer than 30 minutes without supplemental oxygen. The mountains peaked in the San Juan Range at around 13,000 feet. If the plane was on course, these mountains off to the right and left of the planned route reached 11,500, under the elevation requiring oxygen.

The investigator contacted US Customs, US Border Patrol, US and Mexico Intelligence Units and FAA/FSS stations. They all advised on October 28th, between the hours of 1400-1800 no activity was reported in the New Mexico, Old Mexico, or Northeast Texas area. Information regarding aircraft crossing the US/Mexico border reported no activity in that location regarding twin engine aircrafts. The New Mexico State Police felt the aircraft had crashed, as they had never received reports of a hi-jacked or stolen aircraft. McKinley County Sheriff Bass confirmed this information, stating he believed there was no foul play and affirmed the Weyer family was not connected with any illegal activity.

Mr. Gutheinz checked with CAP units, search pilots, ground crews, the High Chaparral Restaurant where Roger and Dewey ate, and local hospitals for any reports of food poisoning. He questioned locals who reported seeing and hearing a twin engine flying north, east of Gallup; another sighting came from the White Horse Trading Post, a twin was seen heading northeast toward Alamosa. The only other reported sighting was between 4-4:30pm near Salida on the east side of Monarch Pass: an aircraft then flying low turned north on the west side of the pass. In an interview with Frontier Airlines Captain Jack Howell, the pilot reported heavy icing conditions when flying in the Gallup area two days before and after October 28.

In my telephone conversations with the investigator, I suggested we pursue the possibility the pilots could have become asphyxiated from fumes. He contacted Wichita Beech Aircraft Corporation requesting info regarding the propeller anti-icing system on the 1965

Beechcraft Baron. He also requested a sample of the embalming fluid and plastic body pouches used by Rollie Mortuary, and a sample of the deicer placed in the airplane by Atsidi Aviation just before takeoff. When interviewing the mechanic who serviced the plane, Mr. Gutheinz discovered there was a question as to where to fill methanol, the deicer. The mechanic thought it to be in the rear of the plane which required the removal of bodies. After searching the rear to no avail, the bodies were returned, and he searched the front compartment where the fill cap was located. He poured three and one-half gallons from his container but said some overflowed from the funnel. That amount should have run out a vent hole to prevent fumes from entering the cabin during flight.

However, statements Mr. Gutheinz received from Denver Beech revealed if drain holes were clogged or if someone had worked on the plane and failed to replace plugs in the firewall of the aircraft, fumes from the compartment could have leaked into the cabin. These fumes, according to the manufacturer, were flammable and harmful. The warning label on the product was marked: *Poison, may be fatal, or cause blindness; use only with adequate ventilation, avoid breathing vapor.* The manual received from Beechcraft answered another question. The propeller de-icing system on a Baron consists of a three-gallon fill tank located below the floor on the left side of the nose baggage compartment. At least one-half gallon of methanol was spilled there, directly in front of and below the pilot's seat.

The Contacts/Correspondence~

Carol and I continuously tracked down leads and pursued any reasonable idea or suggestion offered. We obtained lists of airports and Fixed Base Operators and mailed hundreds of flyers showing a picture of the aircraft, the pilots' photos, and a request to report any information to local law enforcement authorities.

When Senator Abourezk called to help, I asked if he would contact NASA. I was aware that planes or satellites with infrared sensors could detect downed aircraft. They complied. For a two-week period, the area near Pagosa Springs was covered using heat-sensitive technology, until a major snowstorm moved in. NASA sent me photos of the area, along with regrets that they were unable to detect anything.

At my request, the Senator also pursued the means to obtain a list of airports in Mexico. On December 2nd, I received an apology from him for the time it took to receive the list which was compiled in an Aeronautical Information Publication in Mexico, obtained by the FAA Office of International Affairs, delivered to the Senator's Office in Washington, DC., then mailed to South Dakota. In his letter he wished us good luck in our efforts and suggested he be contacted if any further help was needed. We sent flyers to all midwestern and southern US airports, and those in Mexico listed in the publication that Senator Abourezk diligently and successfully obtained.

MISSING PERSONS

Dewey Dewayne RATHKE

D.O.B. 6/17/35
39 — 5'10" — 185 lbs.
Dark Brown Hair
Brown Eyes
White Male

Roger Earl HLAVKA

D.O.B. 2/5/42
32 — 5'9" — 180 lbs.
Blonde Hair
Blue Eyes
White Male

PILOTS OF: Twin Engine Beechcraft Baron, White/Blue N414K

Flight plan filed from Gallup, N.M. to Rapid City, S.D.

Transporting three bodies for burial. No contact since 10/28/74.

Any information to the whereabouts of the above, contact Meade County Sheriff's Office, Sturgis, South Dakota. PHONE 605-347-2681, Office
605-347-5425 or 347-2301 Nights

CHAPTER 9

Months Pass

The last two months had been extremely stressful, to say the least, exhausting both mentally and physically; yet we still knew nothing more than the day Roger and Dewey disappeared. We were hopeful the new year would provide answers soon; prevent months from becoming years.

The holidays were difficult! Thanksgiving was spent at my parents' home, with my brothers and their families. For Christmas, we all congregated at Hlavka's home. Mary prepared a traditional feast; roast turkey, dressing, mashed potatoes & gravy and corn casserole; plus, the family favorite Czech dish: potato dumplings, shredded pork with sweet sauerkraut; and suet pudding! Roger's parents were amazing. The disappearance of their son and son-in-law was taking its toll on them; yet they were so incredibly supportive, strong, and helpful through it all. They and my parents were our saving grace.

January 7th

On the day of our anniversary, I woke wondering what we would be doing, if Roger were here. It was sunny, although very cold outside, icy and snowy; the same as when we were married thirteen years ago… but rather than celebrating with my husband, I was searching for him! Instead of having fun, enjoying an evening of dining, sipping champagne and dancing, I spent the day and night following up on an alarming notice received from the District

Aviation Office, and drafting a letter to Senator Abourezk. The report shared information that numerous aircraft had been confiscated; pilots were being incarcerated for minor infractions on flights into Mexico; FBOs were cautioned to alert pilots flying near the border when making southern flights.

In my letter to the senator, I included a copy of the alert received, an update of our investigation and shared an earlier report received from the District Aviation Office that no radio contact had transpired between FSS or VOR after Roger taxied out at Gallup. I thought it unusual, that *no one* could recall seeing them get in the airplane or take off, suspecting someone *might* have entered the plane to get out of the States and forced them to go south. If this could be a possibility, I asked the senator's assistance in contacting the American Embassy in Mexico and Mexican Embassy in the States. Also, I requested advice on what steps to take in getting all Mexican jails searched. I knew this would probably take an act of congress, but what harm could it do to ask.

January 18th....

All the grandparents came for supper to celebrate Lorie's twelfth birthday and my upcoming thirty-second on the 20th. We had birthday cake and opened gifts; but there were no other surprises, no good news to share. We attempted to put on happy faces, but it was difficult when hearts were hurting. That was the last celebration at the airport house. With income depleting I rented it out, and the kids and I moved to town. Later in January, I received copies of the following letters written to Sen. Abourezk from the State Department and Embajada De Mexico.

Dear Senator Abourezk,

Thank you for your letter on behalf of Mrs. Roger Hlavka concerning the whereabouts of her husband and brother-in-law who recently disappeared. The Department has no information which would indicate they are in difficulty in Mexico or Canada. In order to confirm this, we have forwarded copies of this correspondence to our embassies at Mexico City and Ottawa with the request that they alert all US Consuls in those countries near the pilots' disappearance. We will, of course, promptly relay any information which may be developed by our consular official Kempton B. Jenkins, Acting Assistant Secretary for Congressional Relations.

Dear Mr. Abourezk:

This will acknowledge receipt of your letter of 14th January 1975. Related correspondence from Mrs. Jean Hlavka's matter in question is being transmitted to our Ministry of Foreign Affairs in Mexico, for their attention and possible investigation on the two missing pilots, Dewey Dewayne Rathke and Roger Earl Hlavka, lost on their flight from Gallup, NM to Rapid City SD on or about October 28th, 1974. Should there be any informative reference on these persons' whereabouts, I shall communicate with you in due course.

Yours very truly, For the Ambassador

Lic. Raphael Reyes Sindola
Consul General of Mexico

February 5th...

Roger's thirty-third birthday was a quiet day. His parents invited us for supper. His mother shared happy, fun times and how they had celebrated birthdays at their ranch. She talked about Roger when a child -- how fast he was, winning every foot race he ran and how he always wanted to be a pilot. We laughed, cried some, and hugged each other. Roger's parents were affectionate, not hesitant to give and receive hugs, nor say, *'we love you'!*

February 15th..

The samples collected by Mr. Gutheinz and sent to The Poison Lab, located in Denver, were analyzed and returned with the following results:

> *No chemical reaction between methyl alcohol and isopropyl alcohol; however, methyl is volatile, even more apparent at high altitudes. There was no reaction between the body bag of plastic and Petri Balm embalming fluid. The zipper on the type of bag used does not seal airtight. The most volatile component of embalming fluid is formaldehyde, which is also toxic.*

March 4th....

The investigator received a response to his inquiry questioning whether formaldehyde in the air could interfere with the operation of an aircraft, enough so that it might cause a crash. The report was alarming!

> *There is no question that formaldehyde is so irritating to the eyes and respiratory tree that in significant concentrations in the air, it would make it difficult to see and breathe. These clinical symptoms could be responsible for and interfere with navigation of an aircraft. If the concentration was high, such as could have been the case with three bodies in a confined space, especially if by chance the bag had become punctured or torn from handling,*

the symptoms could be responsible for syncope or even death of the crew.

April 28th

Eddie invited a group of classmates to our home for a dance party on his eleventh birthday. They played records and enjoyed snacks. Grandparents stayed for supper & birthday cake. All the boys stayed overnight. Our situation was on everyone's mind; but not talked about. I had made known to our guests this was to be a happy celebration, that it was ok to have a good time! There was loud music, lots of noise. That was the best part! I wanted to see the kids having fun, to hear them laugh.

May '75

Private Investigator, Mr. Gutheinz, returned an overpayment from the search fund with a very thorough inch-thick report. It included flight plans, detailed interviews, FAA flight rules, toxicology reports, copies of correspondence, 414K's major repairs, maintenance records, registrations & sales records, in-depth financial records, bills of sale, exhibits, photos of Gallup Airport and restaurant, and a final expense sheet. He expressed regrets for not having the opportunity to meet, that he had exhausted all avenues, that his investigation was concluded, his report completed; and thanked us for contacting him. *(newspaper article)*

CAP Unit Resumes Plane Search In Colorado, Gunnison AP

The Colorado Civil Air Patrol reports it is resuming a search for a missing air hearse carrying a crew of two and three bodies being returned to South Dakota. The search for the plane was suspended when a five-foot snowfall hit the Pagosa Springs area, still covered by snow from late last year. The plane was last heard on October 28 and leads the CAP has compiled show the twin-engine Beech Baron could be in the Pagosa Springs area, a spokesman said. The plane was on a flight from Gallup NM to Sturgis, carrying three bodies for a funeral home there. The crew members were Dewey Rathke, 38, and Roger Hlakva, 32, both of Sturgis.

(Letter drafted to NTSB)

June 3, 1975

*National Transportation Safety Board
Administration Safety Division
Accident Inquiry Section, Washington, DC 20591
Attention Chief Supervisor:*

Baron 414K being flown by my husband and brother-in-law was not heard from after filing their flight plan and taxiing out at Gallup. Civil Air Patrols from several states as well as local pilots have searched extensively. We have used AF infrared satellites, and the Embassy has done some checking in Mexico. The CAP will open the search again for a brief time after snow diminishes and before foliage thickens. My sister-in-law and I request that in your publications sent to pilots in the Pagosa Springs area, be encouraged to report all wreckage sights. It is my understanding that this mountainous area holds several known old wreckages captive. Recent wreckages could be mistaken for one of those.

We have also hired a private investigator who has determined there is great possibility that the highly toxic embalming fluid used in the bodies could have caused the pilots to black out which means they would not necessarily have been on their planned course. We would greatly and sincerely appreciate any assistance. If your department is unable to help us, please send this request through the proper channels. Please notify us immediately as to the action taken. Our husbands have been missing since 10/28/74.

Thank You Sincerely!

Jean Hlavka
Hlavka Aviation, Inc.
Hereford Rt, Sturgis, SD

June 9th

Mr. Krueger, Farmington FAA called, acknowledging a request for a list of FBOs in New Mexico. Later that morning, I received a call from Mr. Kapustin, NATSB Wash., DC who acknowledged receipt of the letter below. He offered his condolences, assured follow up on my request which was addressed in the letter, including a Preliminary Accident Report.

June 11th

National Aviation Transportation Safety Board
Washington DC
Dear Mrs. Hlavka:

This is in reference to your letter to the NTSB inquiring about the missing aircraft N414K piloted by Mr. Roger Hlavka, when in route from Gallup, NM to Sturgis, SD on October 28, 1974. Records show that a search was initiated when the aircraft failed to arrive at its destination. The search, however, was unsuccessful and was abandoned on November 4, 1974. A preliminary Accident Report was filed by the Denver field office of the Safety Board on November 6, 1974. A copy of the report is enclosed for your information.

Preliminary Accident Report Prepared 11/6/74

**Pilots: Roger Hlavka-presumed fatal. Passenger: Dewey Rathke- presumed fatal.*
**N414k departed Gallup, NM at 1547 mst on a VFR flight to Rapid City, SD.*
**A VFR flight plan was filed prior to departure.*
**The pilot was offered a weather briefing by Gallup FSS.*
**Purpose of the flight was to transport three bodies to RC for burial.*
**Flight plan route Farmington, NM, Alamosa, CO, Rapid City SD.*
**1555mst weather for Gallup was 1200 broken, 2000 broken, 7000 overcast visibility 2miles, temp 48 degrees, dewpoint 390, wind 2300 at 13 knots*
**Rain unknown intensity south through southwest.*
**A search was initiated when the aircraft failed to arrive at its destination but unsuccessful and abandoned on 11-4-74 due to lack of leads.*
**The air search was centered in the San Juan Mountains.*
**Several feet of snow have fallen subsequent to the disappearance of 414K.*

We very much appreciate your grave concern and feelings in this matter and regret that we cannot be of more direct assistance to you. We do not have a publication that is routinely sent to pilots; however, the Federal Aviation Administration does issue alert notices in conjunction with search and rescue efforts, which are coordinated with the Rescue Center at Scott Air Force Base, Illinois. Accordingly, by copy of this letter, we are forwarding your request to the appropriate officials of the US Air Force Rescue Coordination Center and the Federal Aviation Admin., Washington for whatever action these agencies may be able to initiate.

Sincerely yours,

Bernard C. Doyle, Chief, Investigation Division, Bureau of Aviation Safety cc: Headquarters ARRS/ARBC. Mr. Donald E. Kemp, Chief Accident Investigation Staff Federal Aviation Adm, Wash, DC

(Letter received from the Dept. of Transportation, Federal Aviation Adm)

Dear Mrs. Hlavka:

I have just received a copy of the NTSB letter of June 11 to you in which Mr. Taylor referred to an FAA Alert Notice procedure. The Special Alert Notices referred to, were issued by the FAA, Rapid City Service Station on October 29, 1974.

Their notices are sent via teletype and received in the FAA Communication Centers, including the Military Search and Rescue Groups and various Civil Air Postal Wings or the area of intended flight and for some great distance either side of the intended flight path. We note with interest the missing persons' specifications or information page you sent to the NTSB. We believe this is a good plan and perhaps if you have not already done so, it would be helpful to mail it to the fixed-base operators and the airport managers near the intended route of flight.

While all the above information may be of little assistance to your more direct efforts, we do recommend to you our FAA General Aviation District Office Inspectors located on the Municipal Airport RDSD. The Chief of that office, Inspector C.A. Martineau, is especially qualified in all matters pertaining to general aviation. Please feel free to call on or visit with them. We extend our sympathy to you and Mrs. Rathke in this matter.

Sincerely, Donald E. Kemp

Chief, Accident Investigative Staff
Flight Standards Service

(Letter received from the Department of Aviation State of New Mexico)

Dear Mrs. Hlavka:

Mr. Kreugher, Farmington FAA tour chief, has told me that you wish for a list of FBOs. Enclosed is a list of New Mexico operators. If we can be of any further assistance, please feel free to contact us.

Sincerely yours,

William E. Mekeel, Assistant Director

CHAPTER 10

The Psychic

After everything that had been done when pursuing so many suggestions, leads, and ideas throughout the last ten months, all efforts to locate our husbands had failed. But still, we were not willing to give up. We needed answers, confirmation! The children deserved some form of finalization to end this nightmare. Perhaps this would never come to be. How could we deal with that?

As a last resort, we agreed to consider what friend John Eddy had been urging us to do. After gathering information on the internationally known psychic and learning of his success in locating missing aircraft and solving crimes for law enforcement, I contacted Mr. Peter Hurkos. He agreed to see us; but was hesitant he could locate a plane that had been missing for so long. Regardless, we decided to chance it!

On August 3rd, 1975; Carol, Coke, and I flew by United Airlines to Burbank, California where we were met by Fred Gross, personal attendant to the psychic. He drove us to the Beverly Hills home of a gentleman appearing to be in his early sixties, spoke with a strong Dutch accent and resembled Peter Falk *(Columbo)*. He welcomed us into his attractive Mediterranean style home, introduced his young wife Stephany, and sleeping baby daughter; then invited us into his living room where several of his original oil paintings

decorated the walls. I presented him with a money order in the amount agreed upon for the two-day consultation. Peter first told of his clientele which included an impressive list of movie stars, business and military heads including friend, General Omar Bradley, and several others such as us. He asked if we brought what was requested, then Mr. Hurkos shared amazing insight.

At his instruction, I placed a photo face-down in front of him. Peter put his hand on it, and without hesitation described a blue-striped, white airplane with numbers four and one…the Baron which Roger and Dewey were piloting! He seemed confused, and kept repeating *"two, two"*; then he looked at Coke and asked, *"Two, were dere two?"*

Coke replied, *"Yes, there were two pilots."*

The psychic agreed, *"Yah, en von teach."* When continuing to focus on Coke while making spinning motions with both hands, he questioned him again, *"Two, dere are two?"*

Coke confirmed, *"Yes Peter, the plane is a twin-engine with two sets of propellers."* Then, Mr. Hurkos seemed to understand his confusion, and responded, *"two… boot only von vurking!"*

When asking of something belonging only to the pilots, I gave him a watch that Roger sometimes wore, which Peter held in his left hand. Instantly with a loud verbalized, "voom", his right fist simultaneously came down onto the top of a coffee table directly in front of him… *"he git vurked up, ohfur it kvickly…. he laff, hass fon."*

Peter was right on! Roger, when excited or ticked would *'spout off';* say whatever was on his mind, instantly be over it, leaving you upset and him wondering, *why?* Then throw an arm around you, give a hug and laugh!

Then out of the blue, Peter questioned me. "Baytty, whose Baytty?" Caught off guard I frowned, thought for a moment, then told him I didn't know anyone by that name.

"She nut rumontic, but 'round often'… haf dotter close to you husban; you en he haf two shildran", Peter informed me! Then spoke of a recent partnership, involving land. Roger, and lawyer friend Dale Morman, were indeed purchasing real estate, and had recently invested in a farm they sublet. Naturally, I had interest in knowing more about this *'Baytty' person and her 'dotter'!* Then shortly, it came to me. Oh, of course, Betty! Should have known; but how did Peter pick up on that!! She managed a popular local restaurant in Sturgis,

where her three daughters served as waitresses. One, although married, saw herself as the *'hottest thing in town'!* She thoroughly enjoyed teasing, flirting, and enticing all the businessmen; including Coke, Jerry, and especially Roger, who practically lived there, eating meals, and having coffee daily!

Then, Peter looked back at Coke, *"You haf two shildren, no? A boy en girl? Til wife to see ductor, haf truble, nut serious, boot see ductor.* Coke remained silent, just nodded at Peter in amazed confirmation at all he had been told and heard; and *'knew to be true'!* Then, Peter addressed Carol; *"You haf somting"?* She handed him a pocketknife, which he placed in the palm of his hand.

Peter spoke of cattle and a new airplane. As he continued to describe her husband's recent doings, Carol, with raised eyebrows and tightened lips pressed into one cheek, glanced over at me. I returned the gesture with an astonished shrug. The three of us had been skeptical when deciding to consult him, but Mr. Hurkos had convinced us that he did indeed possess special abilities! In addition to the group reading, he met privately with each one of us, stating personal facts of which he could not have had previous knowledge. But we were eager to gain information we did not already know!

He asked for photos of the pilots which were placed face down on the table with other items belonging only to Roger and Dewey. Immediately, when putting his hands on them, abruptly announced, *"det... boat det".* I thought, but only for a moment, before realizing he was not referring to finances! He continued, *"instontly det, dit nut know, dit nut see da muntin!"* He struck his fist into the palm of the other hand, and emphatically stated, *"Yes, cud nut see da muntin, hit da muntin! Det!"*

He asked for the aeronautical maps requested, laid them out on the floor, taped them together and pinpointed areas where several wreckages had been found. He informed us he would work during the night in darkness, the same as when he paints. We were to return the following day; hopefully by then, he would have something.

That evening, Mr. Gross escorted us to a highly recommended restaurant for its excellent fresh seafood. It was, but I was disappointed when sighting only one movie star. It was Murry Hamilton who played the mayor in Jaws and Mr. Robinson in The Graduate. He was seated at the bar as we entered the restaurant. I acknowledged him, and explained we were visiting from South Dakota. When politely asking him for his autograph, in his highly intoxicated state he belted out a hostile string of slurred four-letter words preceding, *"you goddamn fans!"* That convinced me he shared the same personality as the characters he portrayed in his movies, unlikeable!

The next morning, we looked at the large map where Mr. Hurkos had laid it the night before. Black dots were strategically placed in a mountainous area east of Pagosa Springs, one marked with an X. He asked for complete quietness as he reviewed the map. When noticing where he was focusing, I broke the silence to explain the X he had circled, was much further north of the chosen route, and pointed to one he had placed directly in line with the flight plan filed, *"What about...."* I started, but Peter stopped me.

"No-no, code, defenetley code," he insisted and proceeded to point to other dots on the map, *"Von dare, anotter von dare...boat code!"* I admired his display of paintings while passing through the dining room on our way out. Peter stopped me, *"You like my vurk? Choose von, for you."* He thanked us for contacting him, *"Call me ven de group search."* He took a painting off the wall, handed it to me with a typewritten report.

Aircraft approximately at 9,800 feet, there was bad weather, heavy winds, freezing temperature.

The crash was caused by an oil leak, the plane lost altitude, and was flying on one engine. No survivors. The aircraft wreckage is within 5 miles of an old shaft (mine), about 100 feet away from creek in the mountains. The spot is marked on the map, near Holzwart Ranch and Colorado River. Please see map and sketch attached.

When arriving back at our motel, I protected the large, framed canvas painting in bubble wrap and cardboard, placed the folded map and Peter's report in my suitcase, and waited for Mr. Gross to deliver us to the airport. I purchased insurance on the painting, checked it with our luggage, settled into my seat, and reflected on our sessions with Peter; hoping he was right about where he was sending us, but praying he was wrong about the one thing he felt with absolute certitude!

Once home, Carol and I met with friends who were organizing another caravan road trip to Colorado. A few days later, we and my father set out with the group to a campground in the area near where Peter thought the plane to be. We drove trails and narrow paths when possible and walked the impassable areas. During this time, I checked in with Mr. Hurkos, who had no further helpful insight. Two days later, I returned home with my father, discouraged and disappointed. After our flight to California and trips to Colorado my spirit was at its lowest, in need of energy. We were out of ideas and had exhausted all our efforts. Needing to concentrate on something different, something uplifting, something positive; something besides searching for answers, I decided to give my mind a break! Then, thought of what I had been wanting to do, but hadn't: explore the Ferguson and Hlavka family histories to refresh my knowledge of the hardships *they* faced! Perhaps, learn from them, draw strength from their endurances.

CHAPTER 11

Tracing Ferguson Trails

Tracking the extensive trail of forefathers began with my great grandfather, Monroe Ferguson. His parents came to America from Scotland. Born in 1863 at Rochford, Illinois, he married young at age fifteen. His wife, Jane McFarland, was six years his senior. Her parents immigrated to America in the 1840s from Ballymoney Parish, Antrim Ireland. Tradition has it that Jane's great grandmother was Lady Mansfield of Scone Castle near Perth, Scotland. So... in a distant roundabout way when referring to my grandson as a 'little prince' and granddaughters as 'princesses'… they truly are!

Monroe came to Dakota Territory in 1880 from Rochford, Illinois with his father-in-law, James McFarland, by stagecoach to Deadwood, and applied for a homestead adjoining his in-laws in the Morris Creek, Pleasant Valley vicinity. Jane later joined him, with their two babies Charlie and Wesley, my father's father, who traveled by train from Illinois to Nebraska, then by Sidney Stage to the Black Hills.

The Fort Pierre-Deadwood Trail had newly opened across Sioux Indian lands. The 1877 Treaty gave permission for pioneers to use the trail. Even so, occasional bands of hostiles who had not surrendered still attacked travelers, regardless of any treaties. Problems had flared up with the Sioux. Others who had previously made the same trip, told of camps that had been pilfered by Indian scouts. The intruders would rip open boxes and take the travelers' food and much needed supplies.

An amusing story is told of three scouts who approached the stagecoach on which Jane, her young sons, and sister Alice McFarland were passengers. One helped himself to a pair of red boots with copper toes, purchased in Sioux City, Iowa for their younger brother George McFarland. Enraged, sixteen-year-old Alice grabbed at the boots, beneath the scout's arm. The others thought she would be killed on the spot! Instead, the Sioux warrior just laughed at the young girl's audacious bravery and handed back the boots!

The Sidney Stage continued its perilous route across South Dakota prairies and arrived in the Black Hills without further incident. Monroe and Jane had three more children and lived in the Elk Creek area near Piedmont, raising stock for several years before they, and each of their sons staked homestead claims near the Elm Springs and Creighton, South Dakota areas.

Monroe was credited with building the first dugout dams in those areas and setting plans for an irrigation project. He built a very large log home, part of which was used as a schoolhouse until one was built a few miles from their place. He played violin and, with other local musicians, provided music for dances which oftentimes were held in their home.

Warren and Bessie Stuart Harwood, my father's future in-laws and my other great grandparents, came to the Black Hills by stagecoach from Hudson, South Dakota. Their reason for heading west was due to Bessie's poor health; however shortly, at age 36 she passed; leaving her husband to care for their five children; one, my grandmother Ethel, was ten at the time. Warren moved his children to eastern South Dakota where his wife's sister cared for them, while preparing his Elm Springs homestead for the children's return in 1904. Ethel, now a young lady of sixteen, met and married a tall, handsome young cowboy, Wesley Ferguson. They lived in the Elm Springs area for a few years where their two oldest sons, my Uncles Paul and Frank, were born. Later, they moved to their homestead near Creighton, South Dakota where Wesley built a log home hewn from cedar gathered from the nearby Cheyenne River breaks. There, youngest sons, Uncle Glen and my father Earl, were born.

Wesley and his brothers, as enterprising young ranchers sold livestock to incoming homesteaders settling in the area. When big cattle companies began taking over vast acreages of land, they rode herd for them

and helped with large roundups. With husbands away for lengthy times, the wives were left holding down the forts. For income, they churned butter and delivered it, as well as garden produce and fresh eggs, to Railroad Headquarters in Phillip, South Dakota; a seventy-five-mile round trip, which traveling by horse and buggy took most of the day.

Ethel, a self-taught natural musician, played piano for dances with Monroe, her father-in-law. Shortly after the death of husband Wesley, who passed from pneumonia and flu complications, she began sharing her talent with youngest son, three-year old Earl, instilling his love for music. Son Paul, twelve at the time, took on the role as man of the house, surrogate father, and protector. The three others attended school one-half mile from home. This is where my father's musical interest piqued when teaming up with his teacher. He was the chosen one to pump pedals while she played an old ornate organ; together the duo provided accompaniment while the others sang.

Placed in the middle of a desolate, windblown, barren prairie with four boys, animals, and a farm to tend, Ethel remarried. The worthless drifter was mean and certainly not the husband; nor, the father figure she hoped him to be! Their marriage didn't last long. The boys greatly respected their hardworking mother and loved her dearly. At age sixteen, unable to tolerate her mistreatment, backed by his younger brothers and his trusty Winchester, Paul chased off this hateful man, who ran like a scared rabbit being hunted for the supper meal.

Ethel and her band of boys moved to Sheridan, Wyoming for a few years to be with relatives; before returning to the White Owl/Enning community in South Dakota where dad finished grade school. At the encouragement of his mother and older brothers to continue his education, he agreed to attend Stoneville High School. Shortly, his best friend Bud Funk, provoked by hoodlums to fight; was knifed, and became permanently paralyzed.

Feeling disillusioned with school, disheartened from his friend's condition, and wanting to contribute to the family income, my father quit school. As a young ranch hand, he found employment working cattle and breaking horses at the Slim Cordes Ranch, near Elm Springs, South Dakota. At sixteen, fudged his age a bit, and joined the CCC, building roads and dams that still function in the Black Hills today. The Civilian Conservation Corp was a work relief program from 1933-1942 for unemployed, unmarried young men between seventeen and twenty-eight as part of Roosevelt's "New Deal."

Gifted with an inherent musical talent and passion for music, Dad taught himself to play a variety of instruments *by ear*: harmonica, guitar, fiddle, saxophone, and banjo without the ability to read music; His instruments of choice were fiddle and tenor sax. When playing for dances, all he needed to know was which key to play in and hear the first note of the song. In his teens, he and Mrs. Mildred Anderson, a gracious neighbor lady, dear friend, and excellent pianist, began providing music for dances.

They learned all the latest popular tunes, by listening to the radio and provided music for many years; mostly in cold, unevenly heated community halls. That, and overuse began taking its' toll as Mildred's fingers and knuckles became terribly gnarled from painful rheumatoid arthritis. Even so, late in life, she could still play beautiful music for my father and me when making regular visits to her home in Sturgis.

Knowledge of my mother's ancestry is limited. Her maternal grandfather, Nels Steward immigrated to America from England; her paternal grandfather, Mark Hopkins came from Norway. The Stewards and Hopkins families first settled at Estelline north of Sioux Falls before moving west and staking claims at Plainview, SD. There, my mother Mary Lucile, her older brother Ray, and younger brother Don were born to Edwin and Libby Steward Hopkins.

As a self-professed tomboy, mom preferred being outside with her father and brothers harvesting, haying, hauling water and wood, with a team of horses; unless her mother (whom she called 'maw') needed help inside with cooking and canning. After graduating from

Faith High School in 1933, she enrolled at Black Hills Normal in Spearfish, South Dakota, obtained a one-year certificate, and returned to teach at the Plainview School which she attended as a child.

She, and her life-long friend and fellow teacher Libby, were often escorted to country dances by Libby's brother Ed and wife Mary Hlavka. mother's closest neighbors. It was at a dance in Creighton, SD; where they introduced their schoolmarm friend to the tall, handsome gentleman *'honking his horn'* on the bandstand. *(Incidentally, decades later, the Hlavkas became my in-laws!)*

Our parents were married on Flag Day, 1938 in Sturgis, South Dakota by Rev. C.D. Erskine, well-known and beloved pastor of the Presbyterian Church. They lived near Enning on a small acreage which they farmed and raised livestock until 1945 when mother was hired by Pennington County School District. We moved to Wasta, South Dakota where dad worked for Birdsall Sand Company as a crane operator. By this time, older brother Dale Edwin, myself, and baby brother Wesley Earl completed the family.

We first lived at the old historical two-story Wasta Hotel on main street, confined to a small downstairs apartment; then resettled upstairs into a larger more comfortable one on the back side; away from traffic, with a private outside stairway entrance, and parking space. Later, when becoming available, we moved into a cozy house across from the school near the Railroad Depot.

When freight trains arrived there, occasionally a hobo would show up at our doorstep asking for food or have a water jug filled. Mother never turned them away, would politely have them wait outside while she prepared something for their knapsack. If cold and shivering, she rounded up an old coat or blanket for them. Their appearance frightened me. I would run to hide or stand behind my mother, cling to her dress and peek out at the strange-looking men standing at our door. She had explained they were harmless; just did not have a warm home like we had, but it was right to be watchful. They would always nod, thank my mother, then head toward the depot and climb back into an open boxcar.

It was there, when experiencing the misfortune of being caught in the middle of a vicious dog fight. Kelly, our beautiful long-haired collie resembling Lassie, and I had made our daily trip to the local small-town grocery store. As always, he waited outside while making my usual purchase: one block of Bazooka Bubble Gum. I was busily engaged in removing the wrapper when stepping out onto the sidewalk. Impeccable timing placed me smack dab between Kelly and his bitter enemy, a large German Shepherd. Growling ferociously, they lunged at each other with snarls, curled lips, and wrinkled-up noses, revealing long, pointed teeth. One caught my left leg, and I landed on rough cement between two dogs out of their minds with hatred for each other. With raised hackles, and bloodied jaws they prepared for their next collision!

Instantly, my spindly six-year-old body was swooped up and laid across the arms of a wingless angel --who flew! It was a bumpy ride. With my head bobbing up and down hanging over one arm, and bloodied legs dangling off the other, she raced to my home. I don't remember much of the sprint except for looking up through blurry tears and seeing her pretty face. My savior, neighbor, and high school track star became my hero forever. In all my years have I experienced anything as painful and frightening. To this day I still bear the reminder, a round indentation just above my left kneecap, the size of a large canine tooth!

Later, we moved to a small farm on the Cheyenne River between Wasta and Wall, home of the famous Wall Drug. My brothers and I spent a big share of our childhood there, climbing huge cottonwood trees, playing on sandbars, bottle-feeding bum lambs, caring for our milk cow, chickens who gave us fresh eggs and tame turkeys that controlled bugs, kangaroo rats, harmless garter snakes and huge toads to a minimum. We always knew when the turkeys had something corralled. They made a loud *perk-perk* sound with their heads cocked and formed circles in prancing side-stepping unison around their captures.

Our home was a large comfortable two-story house, previously occupied by a doctor. Beautifully carved French Doors with glass panes separated one room from the others. The doctor had used it as a waiting room for patients; for us, it was a fun place where dad held practice sessions with musician friends. Sometimes, they permitted me to pound the base keys on the piano pretending to be a vital part of the band. That must have driven them nuts, especially the pianist! If so, I was unaware of any annoyance caused. They tolerated me, for which I am grateful. Their endurance instilled my love for the piano.

That is also…where I experienced the burning sting of a BB Gun. With all the amenities the beautiful home had to offer, like most houses built back then; it lacked the convenience of having an indoor toilet! My brother was using the 'outhouse' as target practice; when I stepped out, concentrating on buckling my bib overalls. Either Dale was a very poor shot, off his mark; or was deliberately waiting for me to exit. At any rate, it was a direct hit to my backside cheeks! Until his dying day he claimed it was purely accidental. He never convinced me otherwise!

It's amazing; but that incident and my dog bite are the only two 'injuries' I remember receiving throughout my childhood. I am thankful, they both could have been much worse …if not for 'lady luck'. After being peppered with steel pellets, I still had eyes; *and* escaped from beneath two fighting, crazed wolf-size dogs, out of their minds with hatred for each other; without having my scrawny legs chewed off!

While at Wasta, as well as all the other places we lived, Saturday night dances were our main source of entertainment. Dad was usually in the band providing music; but always took breaks to dance with mom and me. When very young, he held me and placed my hand in his. As I grew taller, we would tightly hold hands while I stood on the toes of his shoes; eventually he taught me how to use my own two feet!

We always accompanied our parents to these events which continued well into the wee hours of morning. My brothers and I lasted until midnight, when everyone went to the basement to consume ground beef or scrambled egg sandwiches, and delicious homemade cakes. Then, we crashed onto warm army blankets that mom placed behind the antique upright piano; the likes of all others that gracefully dominated the stage of every countryside community hall.

CHAPTER 12

River Rats

Cheyenne River Lodge Earl Ferguson on rearing horse, posing for Tourist.

When the opportunity arose for our parents to purchase the Cheyenne River Lodge, we moved a short distance north where they operated a cafe, gas station, sleeping cabins, and campground, located on heavily traveled Highway 14.

My brothers and I loved our new home, living at such an exciting, busy place; and enjoyed all the hamburgers and malts we wanted. Dad was a great short order cook; his hamburgers were delicious; mom made tasty side dishes, coleslaw, potato, macaroni, jello salads and did most of the deep cleaning. They both washed lots of dishes, constantly scraped and cleaned the grill! We were not allowed behind the counter, or in the kitchen, would be in the way; nor was it safe for kids to be around open burners, boiling pots, and hot sizzling grease! Dad mostly operated the gas station himself: filling tanks, changing oil, washing windshields, and repairing tires. The boys spent a good share of their time there; helping with cleanup, fetching and putting away tools, while learning how to maintain and identify all makes of vehicles.

On our many trips to Rapid City or Wall for appointments or purchase supplies, we played *name that car.* Each would pick our favorite make. The boys always had the advantage when choosing 'Ford and Chevy! I was left to choose between one of the least popular makes; Buick, Chrysler, Cadilac. Most of the time the boys won; except when we played the game according to color, when I got to pick all shades of red, including pink. Mom thought it only fair that I should win, *s*ometimes!

I helped in the café by sorting silverware, refilling napkin holders, salt, pepper, sugar shakers, ketchup and mustard squeeze bottles. When assisting mom launder sheets, press them with a roller mangle, strip and remake beds in the cabins with fresh clean blankets, pillowcases and sheets; she made it seem like fun! By playing silly games, speaking Pig Latin, singing *'Twinkle, Twinkle Little Star'* in *authentic* Latin, and reciting the alphabet backwards, rapidly; she made work seem like play. That was the teacher coming out in her!

At the Lodge, we no longer had animals and poultry to care for, or other responsibilities as when on the farm. Having to make our beds, help sweep up, care for our dog Joe and horse *'Shorty'* were our only required chores. We spent most of our time goofing around, especially during tourist season when not in school. We were not bad kids, nor angels; never deliberately looked for trouble, just had a lot of time on our hands, with excessive energy! We especially liked showing off to our closest neighbor friends, Jimmy, Linda, and Kitty Sieh when they came to visit; and of course…. *pestering tourists!*

We would climb a ladder to the cafe roof, hide behind a two-foot extended false wall and wait for travelers to use the outdoor toilet directly below our secret hideaway. It was so much fun seeing them rush out, tugging at their britches while trying to figure out what the heck was going on when hands full of rocks were launched onto the tin roof above them. When feeling brave, we would leap upon the toilet, make a few rapid stomps; and quickly retreat. We also liked setting up dad's microphone and speaker system on the upper level open-front porch of our home; would stay hidden and mimic authentic wild animal sounds, when hikers passed by. This was especially effective at dusk, after sharing with them sights of wolves, cougars and coyotes living on nearby riverbanks. It was funny, watching how fast they could hightail it back to their cabins!

That's where Joe came into our lives. Dad brought the loveable black Labrador puppy home as a surprise; after our beautiful collie died. Joe missed his mama terribly. To keep him from crying, I made a cozy bed in a box beside mine, hung one arm over the edge and attempted to sooth him. This rarely satisfied him. Before long, little Joe was curled upon my chest, where he spent his nights, until shortly becoming too large, and found the floor to be more comfortable.

As he grew older, Joe accompanied us everywhere. The four of us made a great team and were together constantly. He kept rattlesnakes and strangers away, performed tricks dad taught him; was a loyal, faithful companion. We spent a lot of time at the Cheyenne River Bridges located just east of our home, easily accessed by walking, or riding bikes in the ditch alongside the very active highway.

At the farm, the river was different. Shallow, slow-moving streams flowed around large, flattened mounds of sand. That was a safer place to hang out when younger, but as we matured became interested in more exciting adventures which the river bridges provided. Our parents weren't overprotective. I'm sure they were concerned, and at times had reason to be. But they trusted us to use common sense; most of the time we did, *but not always!* Like sometimes, when we went onto the railroad bridge where we hopped from plank to plank and plunked gravel into the river water below.

Usually, Joe perched himself on the bank, watched and waited. He always knew when the train was coming, long before *we did*; and alerted us by barking loudly and circling nervously. However, the last time we were on the railroad bridge, our watchdog had abandoned his post and was off chasing birds in the bushes. We had, as always, placed our ears to the track for an *'all clear'*, a trick we learned from Roy Rogers and Gene Autry movies at the Riata Theater in Wall, South Dakota. Confident we had taken proper precautions, we went about our business goofing off, which we did quite well!

The train's engine was entering at the far east end when hearing its' mournful whistle. To the west, trestles continued to dry ground below, but that was a long jump! Wes & I probably could have made it there, if we ran; but no doubt one of us would have tripped and got a foot stuck between the open planks. Nor were we brave or strong enough to climb down onto a concrete pillar as Dale had done. So, we straddled slantedstruts, attempted to plug our ears while clamping ourselves to the cold, rusty metal and shook from a combination of fear, and extreme vibration. With its loud whistle screaming, the train slowly rumbled past as we clung tightly, until the tail end of the caboose lumbered onto the open track. That scared us! So much so, that we vowed never to go on the railroad bridge again!

Unbeknownst to us, that decision had already been determined. By the time we arrived home, railroad officials were seated in the cafe, having coffee and a serious chat with our father. That's when we received the longest lecture on how to use the good sense God gave us, and most painful punishment! We were barred from going to the river for three months. That was pure torture, surely to be the most boring summer ever! However, that wasn't the case. Our parents got us involved in more positive activities. The boys attended basketball camps, I attended a 4-H and bible camp; and began taking piano lessons from a nice lady and excellent teacher, Mrs. Ruth Bruce.

We were lucky; none of us received serious injury or broken bones during our Cheyenne River adventures. I remember only one slight mishap. Dale and I, being older, paid more attention than Wes. It didn't help that he wore thick glasses. I always thought they were the result of when; a large older neighbor girl sat on his head! I was probably wrong, but that's what I blamed his bad eyesight on.

His glasses were always lost, broken, or taped together. It must have been one of those reasons which caused him to slip off the narrow, one foot raised cement walkway, butted up against the metal railing on the highway bridge. When falling, a small sharp-pointed object, either a rock chip or piece of glass, punctured his head. Instantly, short arched streams of bright red blood spurted with steady rhythmic regularity. Dale picked him up and began running. I did my best to keep up, had to. I thought for sure our little brother was dying! Joe, on the other hand, must have decided this odd behavior was some sort of new game as he barked, wagged, and encircled us all the way home. By the time we got there, the bleeding had stopped. Mother made him lay down, pressed an ice pack on his head, and before long he was fine; up and running around!

Wasta was an active place back then, with good people, and several businesses: an auto dealership, motel, hotel, diner, bar, post office, doctor's office, grocery store and corner drug store with soda fountain! The Cheyenne River Lodge/Corral Inn was boom'in… we had so much fun there, were allowed to explore, learn, invent and loved every minute of it! When my brothers and I talked about growing up on cheeseburgers, where we curled up inside tires and rolled each other down a shale hill behind the station, gathered fossils, listened to Jack Benny, Inner Sanctum Mysteries, Fibber McGee 'n Molly, attended high school basketball games to watch Dale play, *as a 7th grade starter*; and rode *'Shorty'* our old black horse, whose only gear was slow…we always agreed. The best times ever, were spent at Wasta, which in Lakota is pronounced wa'stey meaning 'good water'….it surely was!

In 1955, our parents sold their business due to a serious rash that mother developed on her hands and arms, from overuse of harsh detergents and cleaning agents; even though always wearing cumbersome, protective rubber gloves! We hoped our pesky, *'sometimes-risky'* childhood antics hadn't added to their decision; we didn't want to leave! It meant my family would no longer be going to the home of good friends, Chuck and Selma Tines *(pronounced Teenus)*, where they played Canasta for hours. Their three sons and my brothers would run around outside playing *'Cowboys and Indians'*; while I devoted my time entertaining their sweet little daughter, Sonya. It would mean leaving *all* our friends, never seeing them again; forced to make new ones, where we didn't know anybody!

However, we soon discovered Sturgis was a good place to be! There were lots more things to do; like going to Motorcycle Races, could walk to the movie theater, shopping no longer involved driving to Wall or Rapid City; and making friends was easy, everyone was friendly and welcoming. Mother was offered a rural teaching position with the Meade County School District. Dad put his crane operating skills to use at the Titan Missile Base east of Sturgis, until the project was completed; then employed by the US Postal Service as a rural route mail carrier. Dale, a junior, made the first-string high school basketball team, as an eighth grader I got involved with cheerleading and continued piano lessons. Going to school simply involved walking across the street to Williams Junior High, Brown High, and Grunwald Auditorium. Wesley, as a 5th grader attended Erskine Elementary, located just one block north.

We lived in a large white, two-story, two-bathroom Victorian-style house on the corner of Third Street. My three girl country cousins for a while when attending high school, boarded with us in a large upstairs attic area which was converted into a living space. The boys shared a large upstairs bedroom; our parents' room was downstairs, conveniently located at our back door entrance. and next to the kitchen. Joe got dibs on the living room couch! I shared the other upper bedroom with Grandma Libby after she left grandpa; and until an attached apartment became available, where she resided next to us independently. I often wondered why my mother and uncles, referred to her as *'Maw.'* I thought it sounded disrespectful; but knew they loved her and treated their mother with honor.

That mystery was solved when we took a trip to Bellingham, Washington. That was the first time I remember meeting my grandpa. He was a jolly, round-faced, robust Norwegian oyster farmer. He took us to the beach; where we waded, gathered live oysters, and taught us how to crack open and scoop them from their shell. It was great fun to be with my only grandpa and learn the answer to my question. The entire time we were there, he referred to grandma as *'maw'!*

I was grateful to him for teaching me all about oyster farming; but more so, that mom hadn't picked up her father's other habits… the usage of strong profanity, and overuse of alcohol. The only time I saw him after that was when he came to visit grandma and us, shortly after we moved into our home in Sturgis. I wished I could have had the opportunity to get to know him better; was saddened when he passed in 1959. He had character, and surely lots to offer; after all, he raised my wonderful mother and knew she loved and respected her father; she named her first child, Dale *Edwin,* after him!

The Ferguson residence was an active place. Joe had access to lots of kids, loved riding with dad in his gravel truck; didn't get to swim much, but soon adapted well to city living as we all did. He lived a good 'dog's life'; received as much love as he gave; but eventually succumbed to liver disease. That was a very sad time! Shortly, dad brought home our first television set. Even though the reception was snowy and all we got was black and white staticky skip, the excitement took our minds off our painful loss.

During high school I took on babysitting, and other part-time jobs. On Sundays, attended the Methodist Church with my family where I watched over babies and the smaller children in the Nursery. Once a week, I and cousin Patsy rose early before school, walked to the downtown Rushmore Ads where we folded and prepared the mailout. I also worked there after school; filing, indexing, and assisting well-known, *colorful* Sturgis personality, Kate Soldat; owner of the printing and office supply business, past Sturgis Mayor, and active community supporter. For a short time, I tried my hand as checkout cashier at Piggly Wiggly, until deciding that wasn't my cup of tea; I preferred being around children! Summer months were spent swimming at Bear Butte Lake with friends, attending country dances, and spending time with cousins, aunts, and uncles at their ranches.

CHAPTER 13

Hlavka History

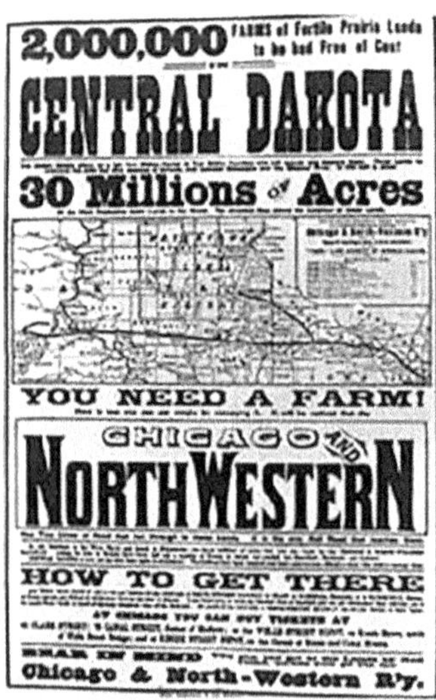

It was posters and newspaper ads, that enticed Roger's grandfather, Frank Hlavka to leave the confusion and hustle-bustle of city life to head out west to Dakota Territory. A contractor by trade, with his wife Anna and two children, were amongst a wave of Czechoslovakian immigrants who came to America and settled in Chicago which served as the starting point for many wanting to explore the wide-open spaces of rural areas. The promise of owning their own land through the Homestead Act, led them west to claim 160 acres of South Dakota's fertile prairie.

The Homestead Act was passed by congress on May 20, 1862, during the Civil War (1861-1865), enacted to secure homesteads to settlers through public domain following the succession of the southern states. As one of the most important laws to ever be passed in the history of the United States, it enabled millions of acres, 10% of the area of the Unit, to be claimed and settled by private citizens. Abraham Lincoln was president then. The Homestead Act was passed by congress in opposition to his lenient plan for reunification of the United States.

Typical Homestead

Early Transportation

In 1908, Frank and his oldest son left Chicago, leaving his wife and other children behind. The two of them journeyed by train to Phillip, South Dakota, then north by wagon, and eventually arrived in Meade County at the newly founded Plainview Trading Post. A Post Office had already been established and relationships with the Cheyenne Sioux had formed, with whom locals exchanged goods. Later that year, Frank's fourteen-year-old son making the same trip as others had, traveled on his own to join his father and brother. Work was well under way on a wood shack, to be completed before Anna and the other children would arrive; however, a powerful twister struck the area, and their efforts were destroyed. Frank and the two boys dug an underground shelter which was their winter residence. The dugout later served as a refuge from dangerous storms and a storage space for food and fresh water. In early spring, the men built a new shack and were ready for the rest of the family who arrived in the summer of 1910.

Life was not easy for settlers on new land where prairie fires, tornadoes, and blizzards invaded their lives. Farming techniques and climate were different in the old country. Forced to diversify, they planted a variety of crops such as corn, wheat, oats, spelt, alfalfa and grass seed. However, there were droughts when nothing thrived. Many of the young men left home to take jobs in more populated areas or worked for aggressive cattle companies who had overtaken large rangelands. Some, discouraged and broke, with livelihoods at risk, returned to urban areas where employment and their future was more promising.

Like many other persistent settlers refusing to give up, Frank Hlavka endured the hardships. After the death of Anna following childbirth, he sent for his wife's younger sister, Eleanor. This was customary, viewed as an obligation for her to care for her sibling's family. She was a brave young lady to travel on her own across the dangerous sea to assume this responsibility. The voyage to America was difficult and lengthy. The conditions had improved, however, with steam-powered ships which shortened the trip. She would also have the luxury of traveling by train from Chicago all the way to her destination, Faith South Dakota, the *'end of the line'* for Milwaukee Railroad.

Frank and Eleanor married and became the parents of four more children. Edward, the oldest, met Mary Mehrhoff, a young lady whose family moved from Omaha, Nebraska and had homesteaded in the Plainview area as well. Ed and Mary married in 1936. Their three children; Carol, Roger, and Bill spent the entirety of their childhood on their ranch near the original Hlavka homestead. This is where Roger became fascinated with airplanes; when at an early age, his uncle Rudd Hlavka took him for his first ride. Living on the wide-open prairie with blue skies the country lad had time to think and plan for when he too, would become a pilot!

Bohunk~

Roger and I met in 1956, as incoming freshmen at Sturgis High. He approached me, bent to read my ID card, and slowly enunciated, *"Jean... Ann.... Fur... gu...son."*

"OK, so you can read," I flippantly responded, while leaning to decipher his identical WELCOME TO BROWN HIGH, name tag. *"Roger... E   Ha...laugh...ka,* I mocked. *"What kind of a name is that?"*

"Bohunk, forget the 'H' it's Lavka; and the 'E' stands for Earl, same as your dad. Call me 'Roj' ... that's more personal. Hell, my folks and yours go way back...they've known each other forever. See ya later; if you're lucky!" He laughed, then continued mingling his way through the large group of enrollees.

I had heard of him... everyone had! He made sure of that. At some time or another, we must have crossed paths, when country kids clashed with town kids at county-wide playdays, spelling bees, or such events. Most likely, we were in the same herd of youngsters with our shoes clamped to rusty roller skates, chasing one another around basement pillars of the Elm Springs Community Hall, while our parents danced on cornmeal-sprinkled floors above. If so, we must not have made much of an impression on each other back then, either!

However, by the end of the year, things changed. The sight of this well-built, blue-eyed country bumpkin dressed in tailored western shirts, cowboy boots and sharp-creased Levi jeans…*began to catch my eye!*

That was enhanced by the fact that he drove his own car, a luxury most high school kids in the late fifties didn't have, unless you came '*from the sticks*' and needed wheels to commute. Maybe it was intuition. or perhaps *someone* had put a '*bug in his ear*', which prompted him to pull up in his '55 blue and white Chevy to a group of friends walking home from the movie theatre and holler, *"Hey, Jean Ann, want a lift?"*

This time, he caught my attention with both eyes wide open! It was difficult, trying to conceal my excitement; but needing to protect my reputation. I hesitated, to impress my friends, and him, *"I am not a 'pickup'!*

Not wanting him to think this was going to be a cinch, I held firm to my '*hard to get*' charade, *"Have to be home in ten minutes, see ya!"*

He laughed, *"That's what they all say! Hop in, we'll take a quick spin around the block, and I'll drop you off!"*

I didn't like the fact that he was so self-assured…or did I? '*Ok, Roj*', I agreed, *"but no 'funny stuff"*. He stepped out, holding the driver's door wide open.

My attempt to execute an impressive slide toward the passenger door failed midway. By the time it took to squish down my grey felt poodle skirt, billowing from layers of *heavily starched cancans*; his right arm had wrapped tightly around my shoulder. Following the traditional drag through Main Street, we continued the short drive to my home. This scenario replayed itself often, whenever he *happened by,* or if I had carefully planned my route. His first kiss was brief, but when a current surged from the top of my pageboy to the bottom of my bobby socks and white bucks, I knew this was more than, *puppy love! (Much more intense; than when innocently holding hands with my grade school 'boyfriend', Johnny Valentine Gravatt, while watching matinees at the Riata Movie Theater in Wall SD.)*

CHAPTER 14

Teen Times/Tying the Knot

For the first two years of high school, Roger lived in town, with his elderly grandmother, Eleanor. After Frank Hlavka died, she remarried and become a widow for the second time; and moved from her ranch to Sturgis. She became well-known to everyone in town as Grandma Stenho, a loving, hard-working little lady with a strong Slavic accent. If excited, she spoke her native tongue, especially to Roger when she knew he was up to *'spatny' (no good)*! She lived in a quaint modest home, with a large yard and huge flower garden which everyone admired. Roger helped her with that and other outside chores. She, in turn, kept him full of delicious Czech food. After school, Roger worked at Ben Franklin stocking shelves until Al Matkins offered him a job detailing cars, cleaning the shop, and assisting mechanics at the Ford Garage. On weekends and during summer months, when not competing in high school bull riding competitions, he returned home to help his parents on the family ranch at Plainview.

In '58, Roger's parents sold their ranch and moved into their new home in Sturgis. He and his younger brother, both nicknamed *'Bohunk'* by their friends, had complete run of the basement where more than a few wild parties took place. Their older sister Carol, was out of school by then, married to Dewey Rathke and had their first of five daughters. Their mother Mary was a wonderful cook, an excellent homemaker, very affectionate and loving. and as a talented seamstress made beautiful shirts for the men in the house. She was the full-time bookkeeper at Piggly Wiggly before employed at Ft. Meade Veterans Hospital as a ward aide with increased pay and benefits.

Roger's father Ed was employed as caretaker/groundskeeper and custodian at Bear Butte after it was established as a State Park and the information center was erected. He built and maintained the original wooden trail which began at the southern base and tracked to the summit of the historical formation; and tended to the small buffalo herd which was brought in to attract tourists. As an accomplished carpenter, he also worked for Leo Wakefield, building homes. Ed was a wonderful person, never spoke a harmful word to anyone, treated his wife like a queen, never raised his voice to her or his children. I thought the world of Roger's parents, they treated me as their daughter; we had a great relationship! Following retirement, they enjoyed summer weekends in their travel camper at Iron Creek Lake, a small Black Hills campground and popular fishing spot for locals, and spent the winter months as snowbirds in Mesa, Arizona.

Roger and I continued our *on-and-off* high school romance, until I attended college in Spearfish, South Dakota at BHTC, as it was known then. Campus life was great. Studying business courses, playing on the women's basketball team, going on extended band and choir trips, meeting new friends, dancing to jukebox music at the Student Union; and being on my own was exciting! During my freshman year, I boarded at the women's dorm, Winona Cook; then on the upper level of South Hall; where boys occupied the lower level, which kept the Dorm Mom very busy, *making sure everyone stayed put in their proper places!*

The Downtown 'Bottle Royal' was the most happening place for chugalugging chanters and jitterbuggers; especially when local musicians Mike Kelly, his sister Bonnie, and Gary *"Muledeer"* Miller provided live music; however, partying was cut short, due to our ten o'clock curfew!

As student secretary, I assisted Dean Kirkpatrick, who often suffered from painful migraines and had to go home, leaving me to manage the office. I also worked part time at a downtown women's clothing shop, was on the football cheerleading squad, Letterman's candidate for Miss BH, and dating a handsome, nice pro-baseball player, who was increasingly winning my heart.

I had the world by the tail. What else could a girl ask for! One would suppose with all that going on, I wouldn't have had time to think about Roj... but did; just couldn't get him out of my head! Impatient to tear the world apart and after a few *'run-ins'* with Principal Bill Brown, Roger quit school, *more likely dispelled*, midway his senior year, and hit the work force. He returned to finish high school the next fall. School was easy for him. He was a quick thinker, did math in his head faster than I could on paper.

It was a weekend home from college, when he came back into my life; and we came to a mutual agreement that we couldn't survive without each other! My parents were not overly pleased with hearing of our decision to get married. They thought we were too young, at nineteen and twenty, and saw Roger as a bit of a *'wild man'*... rightfully so! They thought we should wait -- let him 'sow his oats,' and that I should continue my education, become a bit more mature and work awhile, before making such a permanent commitment. However, their appeal to put our plans on hold fell on deaf ears. Roger was partying but working just as hard, bringing in a good income as a carpenter.

I knew life would not be boring, sharing it with such an energetic, ambitious go-getter...so full of surprises! He was fun, loved to jitterbug; knew all the right moves, and how to make them! His teasing nature, spontaneous laughter, and charismatic personality could get him into trouble; but often, helped him get back out of it!

Tying The Knot~

As a college sophomore, I completed the first quarter and prepared for our wedding, held January 7, 1962. It was an extremely cold day but sunny, when our church, the First United Methodist filled with a large group of friends and family. It was a simple, conservative ceremony with bouquets of red and white carnations decorating the altar and reception area. Matching bows and ribbon streamers were placed at the entrance of each pew. Roger's brother as best man, and five longtime friends serving as groomsmen and ushers, wore black tuxedos. My attendants: a friend and groomsman's wife, a married first cousin, and wild college roommate wore red taffeta dresses, sewn by yours truly; thanks to high school Home Economics class. Our flower girl, Roger's niece Mary Ellen, wore a darling red & white puffy dress.

Accompanying her was Timmie Fenner, the ring bearer dressed like the big boys in his miniature black tux. The two cutest 3-yr-olds ever, easily stole the show.

As we exited the church, rather than facing a shower of rice, we found ourselves ducking a barrage of fluffy snowballs and were captured before escaping to Roger's wildly decorated car. The groomsmen placed me on alternate transportation, a long red wooden sled, and carefully tucked my full-length winter coat around my poufy white gown; the *'borrowed'* in the adage, "Something Old, Something New".

Once seated upon my carriage, they handed the rope to Prince Charming and car horns prompted us to lead the caravan. I did not fall off, nor did Roger fall down; just spun a lot! His slick-soled patent oxfords did not provide much traction on packed ice! It was cold, but a most memorable 'drag through Main'.

For the first year of our marriage, I worked as receptionist/bookkeeper at Sturgis Memorial Hospital. Roger was employed as a carpenter for Shorty Miller, who provided us with our home in Boulder Canyon. Later, we moved into a rental house in Sturgis, owned by John Egger, Meade County Sheriff. On January 18th, 1963 according to her father, *the most beautiful little girl in the world* was born.

When the deputy sheriff/jailor position became available, Johnny offered the job to Roger. First, he had to convince me to agree to the unique conditions of the deal, which meant I would be Jail Matron, chief cook and bottlewasher for prisoners! Against my better judgement, I agreed to visit what could become our home.... the jailor's quarters in the basement of the old historical Meade County Courthouse!

Meade County Courthouse, Built 1894

CHAPTER 15

The Castle Dungeon/ Deputy's Promise

The front entrance to the jail and living quarters was gained by first finding a parking spot, ascending several stone-laden steps of the old courthouse, and opening a heavy ornate wooden door to a landing inside. Stairs leading upward, went to county offices, courtroom and Judge's Quarters. A full flight of wide wooden stairs led to the basement, then down a long dim-lit hallway west to the "Castle Dungeon.'

The back entrance was closer, where a small private parking space was available, unless occupied by Highway Patrol units or police cars. A descent down crumbling cement steps gave way to a large *dingy* furnace room, with washer and dryer. The doorway into the Jailor's Quarters was located directly across the hallway to the south. A few feet away to the west, a heavy steel door with a narrow glass viewing window, guarded prisoners.

The living quarters were a large open space with a fourteen-foot ceiling. Unsightly, drab pee-green painted eight-foot plywood panels reaching part way to the tall ceiling; divided the kitchen, living room and pantry/storage area. To the east, two small areas with fat concrete walls featuring open archways were used as bedrooms. On the west wall of the kitchen, a boxed-off area with a door and lowered ceiling served as the bathroom. The below-ground level residence with a deep window-well off the south wall of the kitchen grew tall stocky weeds, and trash exceptionally well. There, a narrow three by six-foot window heavily guarded on the outside by rusty iron bars, provided the only hint of daylight. One matching this distinctive characteristic, granted prisoners minimal outside lighting as well.

Continuing along with the tour, we were shown a wobbly, uncooperative wooden food cart. When carefully wheeled from the kitchen, into the living room, pushed up a ramp leading west and across the rickety floor of the storage room, it would arrive at its' destination. Welded to a thick wall of concrete separating law breakers from law enforcers, was a hinged one-foot square metal door. It opened to a cubicle for placing food trays. If accidentally left unbolted, a small-framed person could easily slip through the embrasure and with little effort have direct access into the jailor's quarters!

With our tour completed, I stared at Roger, took a long-drawn-out sigh; then offered my opinion. *"You gotta be kidding! Honestly, you really expect me to go along with something so abnormally ridiculous! This is no place to raise babies, you'll be gone all the time, and we'll be left here in this godforsaken medieval dungeon by ourselves, guarding jailbirds! And, by the way…how much would I get paid?"*

"Well…I'll draw a deputy's wage and be gone some; but it'll give you something to do til I get back! You'll be cooking a lot; but it's rent-free, with utilities and meals included!" Roger paused, probably reconsidering he should come up with a better selling point, *"And just think, within a year we'll be living in brand new quarters!"*

I hesitated, thinking it was crazy to even consider such nonsense; but, perhaps, it wouldn't be that bad; there could be some advantages…so, I conceded. *"Ok Papa Bear, I can manage…don't know why I let you talk me into this one; have never broken any laws, but now find myself to be willingly tossed in jail?* Roger, for some unknown reason; thought that to be hilarious; couldn't stop laughing!

"All right 'funny face' 'you win again', for now! If, you sign a contingency agreement! I'll give it one year. You'll be responsible for laundering inmates bedding, at the laundromat, not in our washer and dryer; assist with shopping, hauling in groceries, help put them away. Also, help feed and change crying babies' dirty diapers; and, we will

be living in 'new quarters'! If not, you'll be looking for a different cave partner to den up with; this mama bear and her cubs will be out of here! There is no way that I can keep up with everything this place demands, by myself!"

We had been there only a few months, when on April 28th, 1964; according to his father, *'the most handsome little prince'* joined the reigning king, queen, and little princess at the castle on the hill. I had to agree; our red-faced, big eared, nine-pound baby, was the *cutest* newborn boy, I'd ever seen*!*

Caring for babies, cooking, baking, hand-washing dishes, scrubbing endless pots and pans and wheeling meals to next-door neighbors, three times daily, seven days a week kept me extremely busy; and definitely not feeling very *'queenly'*; but rather worn-out, over worked ... *more like Cinderella!*

Finding sitters for little ones and bad boys next door was something else.... nearly impossible! Mastering the art of handling a stroller, carts full of groceries, and controlling an ambitious toddler through the aisles of Piggly Wiggly became my greatest challenge.

Occasionally, if a female attendant was required when transporting women prisoners, I got a break from my usual routine: that is, if Roger's or my parents were available and willing to keep grandkids and convicts, fenced in! At times when Roger was on the road, out of town; or, if we went out for an evening; Al Matkins daughter Cybil, willingly took over as jailor & babysitter. Most girls her age wouldn't have even considered doing what she did; nor, would most parents have allowed it. But she was a brave, mature for her age, responsible, personable, cheerful high school student who loved children. She was a godsend!

As Meade County Deputy Sheriff, Roger's adventures took him throughout the largest land area county in the state; answering complaints, investigating accidents, traveling to the Sioux Falls State Penitentiary, the Yankton State Mental institution, and escorting inmates to and from similar in-state and out-of-state facilities. He was not home much, but did adhere to our agreement; *with one exception...the diaper thing!* He made a weekly trip to the local laundromat to wash inmates' bedding and hauled in heavy boxes of groceries. However, he had assistance! Trustworthy inmates were always eager to be put on 'work detail'…to get a little sunshine and breathe fresh outdoor air!

It was summer in '64 when the deputy entered the castle dungeon, handed me a bouquet of freshly picked flowers, used his *'throw the arm around a shoulder trick'* and suggested a short walk, *"You and the kids need to get out of this place, besides… it's beautiful out there!"*

Wondering if that was in reference to the great outdoors; suspecting he had something up his sleeve, I quizzed him, *"OK Roj, what's up?"* We had made only a few steps out the back door exit onto a downward path which led away from the mighty fortress when he no longer could contain himself. His announcement gave cause for my abrupt stop, *"You… what??"*

He was excited, like when a child and hearing the roar of the neighbor's approaching plane and standing in the middle of the pasture waving, waiting for the pilot's wing-tip salute. He talked about his childhood dreams often, which on this day had become a reality. He was thrilled! The bank had loaned him funds to buy an airplane and a row of old hangers. Then, he insisted we take a short trip to the airport to view his purchases and meet his instructor, Johnny Johnstone, from whom he had been *covertly* receiving flying lessons for several weeks!

Deputy's Promise~

Watching the new courthouse being built was fun and exciting. When finished, in late 1965 it was awesome. The Deputy had kept his promise! The jailor's quarters were a blessing! They were located just below the sheriff's office, with windows on the east at ground level, a living/dining room combo, a bathroom with shower, two bedrooms *(with doors)* and a modern, convenient, well-lit walk-through kitchen with a dishwasher and adjacent laundry room.

The kids spent hours riding trikes across the hall in a large unfinished area, which eventually became a community room and additional county offices. With no yard to play in, just an active parking lot full of busy vehicles coming and going, the large empty space served as a great playroom. Having full run of the courthouse they had won over all the clerks; especially Carolina Brown, the Clerk of Courts, who became their best buddy. They visited her often, always returning with pockets full of tootsie rolls or other such wondrous goodies!

On one occasion, these treats included a box of jumbo-sized crayons. When they had not returned within the time allowed for *'visinin',* I set out to retrieve them and discovered two little Picassos just outside our door, designing a large mural on the wall as their canvas. For as far as little arms could reach, there were colorful circles, squiggly lines and other peculiar shapes which would have impressed the master artist himself. Intensely involved, they hadn't noticed me staring at them, until hearing my long drawn out, *"Ooooh…oooh ....* *oh my!"*

My three-year-old turned to me and proudly exclaimed, *"Mama… inet bewful?"* Hesitating to critique their artwork, I agreed. *"Yes, it's beautiful, but for now you little darlins, come with me! We need to have a 'sation'.* That is what they called our serious talks! They agreed to give up their crayons for a spell, until the importance of the eleventh commandment: *'thou shall not color on walls ever again, only in coloring books',* was fully understood! After receiving assurance that they would not be placed in *'jayo'* for their misdeed; they helped fill a bucket of hot soapy water, chose a brush of their liking and we scrubbed. It wasn't long into the joint cleanup when, *'I ty-uud'* began. Noticing tiny drippings from their chubby cheeks, I felt guilty, not because they were having to work so hard, I knew their tears were from having to destroy their grand masterpiece. When scrubbing, and successfully removing crayon markings; patches of paint came off, as well! The janitor was not very pleased with us; when having to sand and repaint the entire wall!

The five years with the Sheriff's Department were an eye-opening course in human behavior. Living at the jail, made for interesting conversations. Roger got a kick out of teaching his little toddler what to say when asked her name and where she lived. She talked early, but unable pronounce letters 'L' & 'T' would reply ever so politely, *"Mine name is Ordy, mine daddy awesses pepo en wee wiv in jayo."*

There were heartwarming times when living in jail; but many were sad and *'heartbreaking'.* Two of those times were when at the old courthouse. It was late one evening when a call came in, reporting two women with a young child sitting on the roadside of Highway 34, east of Sturgis. When Roger reached the threesome, he found the adults to be highly intoxicated, trying to hitch a ride to the reservation. The small girl dressed in shorts and a flimsy top was shivering, crying. Her long, dark black hair was matted, her body and clothing stained with dirt, were urine soaked. He wrapped the frightened little girl in a blanket and placed her in the warmth of his patrol car. When an HP arrived at the scene, the uncooperative women were placed under arrest and escorted to the Meade County Jail.

As a jail matron, I thought it reprehensible to lock children in with parents. Usually, they needed to be rescued from them, and such was certainly the case this time! I had filled the bathtub with warm sudsy water and found fresh clean clothes, when Roger brought the frightened child into our home. Excited to see another little girl, Lorie ran up to her and exclaimed, *"Me Ordy, wanna pway??"* The bewildered little girl slowly raised her head and responded with a shy silent smile. She was very quiet, seldom spoke; never gave up her name.

The newfound friends shared a tricycle, a meal, and a warm bed. They rose early, played with dollies, ate Mickey Mouse pancakes, and *'helped'* feed the baby. Mid-morning, the girls hugged goodbye, and Roger carried the small guest upstairs to the sheriff's office where family members were waiting to take the sweet little girl home. Her mother and aunt remained in jail, serving time for public intoxication and child endangerment. I dutifully gave them three meals a day and faithfully escorted them down the hall for their daily shower during their few days of incarceration, which in my opinion, was far too lenient!

Another call left one family devastated, and the officers moved to tears. Johnny and Roger often accompanied each other, depending on the nature of the call, or when both were available. Unlike local police or highway patrolmen they didn't carry handguns, wear badges nor uniforms; usually dressed in long-sleeved white shirts, brown pants or blue jeans. They both knew the entire county like the back of their hands, where to go and the shortest way to get there. This time, they were summoned to a residence at Black Hawk, with a creek pond located near the back yard. It was dusk and getting dark, warning lights of bright colorations twirled, and a blaring siren cleared their way.

When approaching the water's edge, their headlights lit up a figure standing frozen, pointing with one hand, the other clasped over her mouth, not beginning to muffle gut-wrenching wails. Johnny stood with the distraught woman, clearly suffering from shock. Roger threw off his boots & Levis; then entered the water. He could swim, but not well; so, it was good that wasn't required of him. The pond had deepened to his shoulders when he reached for the lifeless body of a little girl lying face down. He turned her over, placed his arms under her tiny body, took her to the young mother; quickly grabbed his pants & boots, jumped in the car, turned on the heater full blast, and redressed!

Unable to hear the child playing in her room as she had been, the mother searched inside their home, calling for her, then searched outside. Panicking, she recruited the neighbor lady's help, and they found the little girl floating in the water. The neighbor rushed to the house, called the sheriff's office, and stayed with a small baby boy sleeping in his crib. The officers stood with the mother clutching her deceased child, attempting to comfort her; while waiting for the county coroner to arrive; then drove to the courthouse in silence. When Roger came through the door and greeting him with a hug; wetness pressed against my cheek, *She was three, that little girl was only three years old!*" When seeing *his* little girl running toward him, wiped his eyes, swooped her high in the air, squeezed her tight against his water-stained shirt; then put her down, patted her head with a *"c'mon sweetie"* and together they went to free the noisy toddler, who upon hearing his father's voice was hollering and violently shaking his crib.

CHAPTER 16

The Jail Break

A typical strong steel door with a small window placed at eye-level separated the new living quarters from the, supposedly *'escape-proof'* jail! Most of the time, I left this heavy door open; that was more convenient, when delivering meals, attending to prisoners and keeping watch on visitors. A wide hallway led to containment units: on the east side was a drunk tank, women's cell, and one for those with behavioral issues; on the west, at the end of the long hallway was a large bullpen with individual cells. Each unit had the same steel door which provided a view of inmates being held behind a wall of iron bars with a sliding section.

When notified that an officer was bringing a visitor down, I retrieved a large metal ring of oversized keys, pulled open the hallway side door which only required a key when entering from the outside. Seeing the visitor was empty handed, *confident he had received the routine 'pat down';* I accompanied him to the bullpen where three inmates were being held. After unlocking the main steel outer door, stepped up to the retractable gate and jiggled it, as always; the same as when leaving home and wiggling the doorknob a second time, to make sure the door is locked.

Insecurity is heightened when operating a home for jailbirds. It's impossible to know which ones are entertaining flight! I became watchful, suspicious, less trusting, and made it a point to know all about each inmate. Aware of why the one being visited was incarcerated; I reached back a second time to verify the sliding gate was secured.

The bullpen walkway separated two rows of open cells with cots, stools, and sinks. Inmates could freely roam about, in and out of their cell with access to the shower stall and to the sliding door which required a key to release but latched automatically when slid horizontally. There, the confined could converse with visitors and through a narrow slot received food trays, tissue, soap, mail, clean bedding, and clothing. The inmates were permitted to wear street clothes, *not required to wear prisoners' uniforms!*

When returning to the bullpen to rid the visitor and serve inmates lunch, I was surprised he had left without informing me, as requested; and *'shocked to the core'* when seeing the inner sliding door, slightly ajar! Instinctively, I slid it back to gain full power, forcefully slammed it sideways and hollered to an inmate sitting in the aisle, leaning on the outside of his cell with arms crossed, watching me. It was irritating, that he had purposely deposited himself in this comfortable position to patiently await my reaction to the situation. *"Damn it! How many are in there?"* At first, he ignored my insistent questioning, then shrugged, slowly unfolded his arms, and held up two fingers. He made no attempt to budge, nor offer any information when I continued with a rash of questions, *"Who's gone? How in the hell did he get out? How did he get this door unlocked!"*

It was his impudent, insolent manner; but mainly his *'chessy cat grin'* and disregard that caused my anger to rise to its highest level, *"Answer me!! It's not my fault you're in this place!"* With a stern, squinted glare, I reassured him, *"Remember sir, it is up to me to decide whether you ever eat again …or not! Now, tell me who is left in there with you!!"* He looked up slowly, gave another sickening smirk as if to say, *'I'm the one in control here!'* He had succeeded in getting me ticked off, and it pleased him! Then, taking his glaring eyes off me, he rolled them in the direction of a fellow inmate in his cell, pretending to be asleep on his cot.

He looked back at me with a proud smug, *"It's just you and me honey; and that guy over there!"* With total disgust I sternly informed him that I was not his *'honey'* and never again refer to me as such, ever! I slammed the outer door, locked it, ran up the hallway and grabbed the two-way, and loudly announced, *"Escapee, Meade County Jail, alleged rapist, visiting accomplice unknown if armed"!* It could have been the extreme rattling of metal clashing into the steel cage or crashing sounds of the heavy outer door vibrating upward to the sheriff's office, or perhaps it was the first word over the intercom that alerted them. I hadn't got much past *'escapee'* when within moments two officers, guns drawn, were at my door; and patrol cars, with sirens blaring, began scattering like a hill of disturbed angry ants.

It was the visitor who somehow jimmied the latch on the sliding gate to free his buddy. Those details were found out in court after both were apprehended a few days later, when other chilling information was shared! The escapee related that he and his friend peered from the main door of the bullpen for some time; watched as I prepared lunch, and the kids make rounds on trikes through the kitchen. When turning to remove food from the oven and dish up trays; they silently slid against the hallway wall, exited the side door, went to the north entrance of the courthouse, passed two unsuspecting highway patrolmen chatting; then outside to the parking lot where they left in the friend's get-a-way car. I was pleased to know that the escapee and accomplice would not be returning to the Meade County Jail; they were transported to the State Prison!

Jailors' Break~

A jail was not the proper environment to raise our children, and Roger's plans to change things were well underway. He had kept Sheriff Egger up to date on our growing business and decision to build our home on land we had purchased next to the airport. Johnny was aware that when the kids were in kindergarten and first grade, we would be leaving; however, the jailbreak at a time when Roger was on the road convinced us to leave law enforcement early.

My father, recently retired as a rural mail carrier and having served as substitute jailor, assumed the position fulltime. He was a good cook and with mom gone teaching, he prepared most of the meals. I'm sure the inmates got fed better after he took over! By the time we left, I was *'burnt out' and fed up'* with *feeding and dealing with unappreciative, belligerent jailbirds!* My parents moved into the jailor's quarters. We lived in their home, while ours was being built near the airport. During this time, I filled in as substitute receptionist, legal secretary for the attorneys in town, and assisted at the Sheriff's Office; until landing a fulltime job as receptionist/dental assistant at Wood and Kullbom Dental. From there, I took a Civil Service exam and was employed by VAH at Fort Meade.

Living at the jailor's quarters worked very nicely for my mother, who could walk across the street to Erskine Elementary, where she spent the last years of her career teaching fifth grade. This was a welcome change from driving miles and hours on impassable, muddy, snow-packed country roads. Parents often requested her. Her classes at Erskine were made up of students needing additional individual help; and those with behavior problems that the younger teachers couldn't handle. She seldom had discipline issues in her classrooms, or as a mom!

I cannot remember a time when she raised her voice to me, did not have to. When she had *the look* and called my name with emphasis on the middle one; I knew she meant business. If her eyes snapped and jaw set, I paid full attention! She was fun, had a dry sense of humor, was patient; but a *no nonsense* mom. On one occasion when driving us to school in Wasta from the Cheyenne River Lodge, my older brother was misbehaving, teasing me and sassing back at mom. She simply pulled over, made him get out and walk the rest of the short distance into town.

When realizing the inexperienced, first-year teachers with college degrees, were earning substantially higher salaries, mom took sabbatical and attended Black Hills Teachers College in Spearfish, South Dakota, where my brother Wesley was also a senior. In 1968, after years of faithfully attending summer school her unwavering persistence paid off, and she finally earned her bachelor's degree! At graduation ceremonies they crossed the stage together hand in hand, to standing applause. Her friends and family were very proud of her, but not surprised; our mother was steadfast, consistent, dedicated, and dependable. An article and photo of the mother/son accomplishment made the Area Graduations and Happenings section in the Rapid City Journal. This was around the same time when she was awarded the honor 'South Dakota's Teacher of the Year'.

Her early years of teaching, like those of all rural schoolteachers, were not easy. After fighting the elements and bad roads, they were with their students 7-8 continuous hours, usually teaching all eight grades. The one-room wood-framed schoolhouses had little insulation, if any; no bathrooms or running water; had wood burning stoves that required constant stoking and refueling with kindling stacked outside. Water for drinking and washing hands was pumped from wells and stored in containers inside. Hot water came from tea kettles atop the stoves. During winter months, when dismissed for the day, the teachers who weren't provided with a teacherage or stayed with patrons, drove home under questionable road conditions—and after dark. The other seasons were easier when teachers didn't have the challenge of trying to teach students with chattering teeth and frostbit fingers. Their biggest concern in the fall was watching for prairie rattlers when denning beneath the building; in spring, it was watching for them when they came back out.

CHAPTER 17

The Waiting

Carol and I continued to follow up on any information received and considered every idea that filtered our way. It seemed an eternity since receiving notification from Flight Service almost a year earlier. Organized searches had been discontinued, outside interest in the missing aircraft was dwindling, and search funds were depleting. Our only hope now was that something would develop from all that had been done, *or* through some type of miracle. Fortunately, Colorado CAP continued to put out newspaper articles from time to time.

<u>Lost Planes Are Sought</u>-Oct 12th, 1975

The Colorado Civil Air Patrol today requested assistance from hunters in locating three missing aircraft. These planes are believed to have crashed in the Colorado Mountains during the past three and one-half years.

The most recent vanished June fourth of this year. The white and yellow Cessna disappeared on a flight between Grand Junction and Akron, Colorado. On board were Doctor and Mrs. Morris Batey and their four- year-old daughter. The Civil Air Patrol conducted an intensive thirteen-day search, could find no trace of the aircraft. Relatives of the Ridgecrest, CA family have offered a $750 reward for information leading to the discovery of the missing aircraft.

Also missing is a white and blue Beech Baron which disappeared last October 28th while on a flight from Gallup, New Mexico to Sturgis,

SD. The aircraft is believed to have crashed in the vicinity of Pagosa Springs. On board the twin-engine airplane were Dewey Rathke and Roger Hlavka Sturgis, SD. The aircraft contained three bodies being transported for burial in South Dakota.

The third missing aircraft is a green and white Piper Aztec which disappeared while on a flight from Denver to Salt Lake City. Piloting the airplane was Jim Drummond of Denver. Hunters who locate aircraft wreckage are asked to contact the Colorado CAP or the state emergency operations center by calling Buckley Air National Guard Base at 366-5363.

Throughout the search, we were often at the Rathkes, spending Sunday afternoons at their ranch where the kids roamed the countryside, rode horseback, and involved themselves in all the fun that farms offer. Eddie wasn't always the only boy; sometimes, Dewey's nephew was there. Two was always better than one, when being ganged up on by tough farm-girl cousins. Carol was a wonderful cook, we would enjoy a deliciously prepared meal, including homemade pie; then play cards or compete in a challenging game of Monopoly or Uncle Wiggly.

A couple of times the kids and I stayed overnight in our cabin at Terry Peak Ski Resort; but it was not the same without Roger. We had purchased the two-bedroom log home when taking up the sport of skiing in the winter of '72. When coming off the slopes and ready to call it a day, we continued downward past the chalet and arrived directly at the door of our cozy little getaway. The kids loved having friends for sleepovers in the open loft; we often invited guests for weekend ski parties and barbecues during the summer months.

However, now with Roger gone, the cabin was a big responsibility. Once, a family of raccoons invited themselves in through the chimney, ate what food they could get to, and messed up everything!! After being informed that a certain someone had obtained a key and was frequenting the place without my knowledge *and* the water company reported pink icicles decorating the outside foundation, I'd had enough. Water pipes had burst and flooded the entire floor; covered with red shag! After giving it a thorough cleaning and changing locks, I put the cabin up for sale!

As summer approached, Carol and I toured the kids through back roads in the Black Hills and gave them rides around town in the hotrod dune buggy that Roger had acquired. Often, all of us joined Ed & Mary at Iron Creek Lake, where we pitched tents, fished from their boat, roasted hot dogs and toasted marshmallows on whittled branches. Occasionally, Carol and I joined up with friends for an evening out.

Mind Time Travels~

To free my mind from working overtime during daytime hours, and when *'searching dreams'* woke me during the night, I pressed my memory to relive happier times, when life was simple! Going there was refreshing, comforting; a secure safer place without worries and disappointment, *when revisiting nostalgic stress-free childhood days.*

I thought about my friend Mary Jane Brennen, when pretending to be ticket agents in uniforms at the old abandoned Wasta Railway Station. Inside, it gave off an odor of oiled wood and sweeping compound that only old depots own. We played in the apartment above, where she and her parents lived. She had cool stuff; dolls I had not seen before and listened to records that told stories while we read along in matching books. Then, we might wander over to a vacant lumber yard and enter the large, rectangle building. We climbed steep stairs up to a railing, looking down onto the empty room with a dirt floor. A u-shaped wooden walkway began at the top of the stairway and wrapped around to a wide pushup door; there we would run from one end to the other, yodeling and hollering quick loud noises, that echoed back!

My other friend, Bonnie Lou Bandy, lived in a large, beautifully decorated home with fancy things, which would have been out of place, in *our home!* Her grandfather was Dr. Heinemann, a wonderful family doctor who kept the whole community patched up and immunized from his office in his beautiful white two-story home, the same as Bonnie Lou's house. She was always nicely dressed, as was her mother, a stay-at-home mom; both were polite, prim, proper; but very nice, always welcomed me to their home. Her hair was always perfect, unlike mine that remained in two long thick braids for several days, then mother shampooed it and wrapped sections on two fingers into long ringlets. When it tangled, lost its' curl, and no longer shiny, the pigtails returned.

Mary Jane and Bonnie Lou were girly, unlike me. Sometimes I wore dresses to school, always to church; but at home, played in worn-out pants and bib overalls. That was more comfortable, and I didn't have to worry about getting dirty. Mary Jane and Bonnie Lou never got dirty. I don't think they had as much fun either; neither had an older brother who could always think of something exciting to do! I often thought of Joe when living at Wasta; the love we shared, and all the wonderful times spent together. That made me smile, sometimes laugh, but always made me happy when going back there, if only for brief moments.

Memorable trips took me back to my most favorite places, one being Uncle Paul's and Aunt Ada's ranch located near Enning, South Dakota. My cousins, brothers, and I caught box turtles at Big Dam; and climbed Windcharger Hill, ran back down pulling silk parachutes that Uncle Frank brought back from a factory in Seattle. We hoped they would give us lift. They didn't, just slowed us down a bit!

North of their large two-story farmhouse, close to a root cellar that smelled of damp dirt, was a small brick icehouse, where thick layers of sawdust and woodchips covered blocks of ice. Aunt Ada would send us there to retrieve it when making homemade ice cream. She could whip up large, delicious meals faster than anyone I knew. She had lots of practice with six kids to feed: Wiley, Virginia, Monté, Frankie, Annabel and Patsy; plus, their friends and cousins! Never was there a time, when at their ranch that were we the only ones visiting them! Invariably, a neighbor, friend or other relatives showed up, usually around mealtimes! No matter how many, Ada always had plenty of food prepared; enough for everybody!

Sometimes my cousins, brothers and I, ventured up the creek to Cut Bank where deep foot and handholds dug into a steep dirt cliff, took us atop to a variety of wild bushes, and our return route back to the ranch. Just south of the house, was a shallow creek where strong wood vines hung over it. Pretending to be Tarzan, we used them as a rope and would swing from one edge of the creek to the other. All we had to watch out for was patches of stinging nettle weeds when landing; and made sure we were back for lunch and supper meals. Ada was strict about that; if late, we didn't eat!

When leaving there in *'my merry mindmobile'*, I would stop to visit Uncle Glen, Aunt Eula and cousin Freddie at their Elm Springs Ranch; where I was often chased by a gander, and played with a pet deer. I might wade in a rocky creek behind their big red barn where Fred's pony *'Midge'* was always agreeable to give rides! My parents, brothers and I were there a lot. Often, Uncle Frank, Aunt Opal and cousins Jimmie & Linda would be there as well; especially when celebrating birthdays, holidays or on branding day.

Freddie collected large marbles, lots of them! My brothers and he played games for hours on their large screened-in porch. There, long wide slanted windowsills provided perfect tracks for racing marbles. Fred would have made an excellent professional racecar announcer; he got us extremely excited, just listening to him call *'marble races!* Not having a little girl of her own, Aunt Eula doted on me. She loved brushing my thick, long hair; and *'let me help'* when preparing delicious meals, and homemade desserts. My favorites were her raisin cream pie, and wonderful four-layered devil's food cake!

Trips down memory lane were my getaway; provided courage and energy to handle the reality my kids and I were facing. Kids…. thank the Lord for kids; what would I have done without them! Thinking of the many happy times we had as a family gave me the greatest strength. They became experienced flyers, traveling with us whenever possible, and occasionally got in on short charter flights.

We took them, at ages four and five, on a commercial flight to Florida where Roger checked out an airline training school. He passed the screening test with *'flying colors'* which included questions regarding etiquette, the proper wine to serve with different types of meats, etc. We gave serious consideration to everything involved and chose to continue doing what we were doing, which was going quite well! Rog was always thinking, always full of ideas. But for now, his thought of becoming an airline pilot would be put on hold. We went for a swim in the ocean, took the boardwalk through the Everglades, Alligator Alley, and toured Parrot Jungle before heading home. Upon  entrance to the bird conservatory, we purchased seeds from a coin machine and wandered around watching and looking at beautiful specimens perched in trees. Near the end of our tour, we were invited to interact with several tame parrots. With her bag of seeds, Lorie began feeding them, Eddie was empty-handed. When asked what he did with his, he responded meekly, 'I giv tum to the boods, and tum to me.' His father took his hand, found another coin machine, and they returned with a full bag of treats so he could feed the parrots, which tour guides had gently placed upon their shoulders!

CHAPTER 18

Conformation/Facing Facts

The one-year anniversary of Dewey's and Roger's disappearance was approaching. Carol and I had discussed that something needed to be done, but what! Neither were ready to make any final arrangements. We kept those thoughts to ourselves, agreeing that would be addressed when the time was right; not until the search was complete, not until there was proof. So, that is how it was; until October 15th, 1975.

The call we had hoped, prayed, waited for and feared; came on that morning at 9 am. The call that finalized the search was from Pagosa County Warden, Judd Cooney. I could tell by the sound of his voice he was not calling to report the miracle we hoped for. *"Thank you, Mr. Cooney, thank you for calling, thank you for everything you've done. How in heaven's name, were they found!"*

There are those who come into our lives as gifts from God and don't know it… but those of us on the receiving end, do! Judd told me about a 65-year-old elk hunter, Mr. Oliver Lane from Odessa, Texas who had been hunting in high country for several days. Early Sunday, on the morning of Oct. 12th the same day as a newspaper article, **_Lost Planes Are Sought_** was published; Mr. Lane was watching a large herd of elk grazing in a deep, rugged draw. Through his scope, he spotted a shiny metal object just below the timberline on the next ridge. He felt certain that what he saw was the tail of an airplane beneath a cliff above; but was unable to get to it due to harsh terrain. It took two days for him to work down off the mountain, and report the sighting to Warden Cooney, in Pagosa Springs.

At first, the authorities thought it to be an old wreckage; however, at the persistence of Mr. Lane who pinpointed on an aerial map what he saw, flew with search pilots for two days before locating the wreckage. Practically impossible to see from the air, it was visible only momentarily if directly above it. On Tuesday, traveling by horseback for three hours, then two miles on foot, Mr. Cooney, Bill Richardson from the District Attorney's Office, with Mr. Lane guiding them, arrived at the wreckage identified as Beechcraft Baron 414K containing logbooks belonging to Roger.

The men completed a preliminary investigation and Warden Cooney shared that he and Sheriff John Evans would be returning to the sight to complete an official investigation. The warden and I had kept in contact with each other. Shortly after meeting him in November of '74, he felt that if the plane was found, it would most likely be by a hunter. I thanked him sincerely, "You were right, Judd, thank you, thank you!"

"Yes," he agreed, "Thank God for hunters, that's usually the case, but most of the time it takes much longer. I'll include Mr. Lane's address and number with other information I'll have for you later this week." I thanked him again, told him how much we greatly appreciated him and his officers for helping with the search, and would be anxiously waiting for his report and any other information available.

Facing Facts~

When starting to dial Carol, I was overtaken with mixed emotions. Loud gasps and shaky, shallow breathing elevated to uncontrollable sobbing! Was it relief, or *grief!* Who would know, but it felt good to cry. I repeatedly thanked God, but for what… knowing for sure that seven children were indeed fatherless? It was pure torment not knowing anything! At least now, *we knew*, and were forced to release the last shred of hope that lingered. The search was finally over, still there were so many unknowns; but needed to start thinking clearly, deal with questions later. For now, I was thankful for prayers answered, for Mr. Lane, the one person who was in the right place at the right time, and for all the hundreds of others involved in so many ways! Then, as quickly as the emotional shroud came over me, it lifted.

After calling Carol, I placed calls to Marty, my in-laws, my father; then the school and asked for my mother. When I pulled up to Erskine Elementary, the children were on the front steps with their grandma's arms tightly wrapped around them, waiting. They had their share of waiting, waiting for answers, waiting for their daddy. Now I had to tell them something I had hoped they would never have to hear; and did not know how or what to say! The minute they got in the car, all they had to do was look at me to know why I came to get them. I explained it was going to be difficult without their father; but we had each other, and together with their grandpas and grandmas; *somehow…*we would get through it. I hugged them, and we drove home in silence. Shortly, all their grandparents arrived.

Throughout the past year, I had tried to prepare them for the worst, but how do you tell a child something you don't know! We had talked, cried, wondered, prayed, worried, feared, hoped; but did not laugh much. Not knowing destroys the spirit, leaves little room for joy and happiness. But now, we knew.

I was anxious for the dullness in my children's eyes to disappear; to sparkle again, and the darkness beneath them vanish. I wanted to see their big wide-mouthed smiles, to hear their laughter; but that would take a while.

Article appearing in the Pueblo, Colo. October 17, 1975, newspaper

<u>Hunters Find 2 Missing Planes</u>

Authorities recovered the remains of eight persons from the wreckage of two light planes, one of them nearly a year old. Both planes were found by elk hunters during their wanderings through Colorado's rugged high country. Three members of a California family were found in the wreckage of their private plane eight miles southwest of Hideaway Park. The victims were the pilot Dr. Morris Baley, 34, of Ridgecrest, CA., his wife MaryAnn, age 37, and their daughter Michelle, 4. Their Cessna 172 disappeared from radar screens June 4, 1975 while on a flight to St. Paul, Minn. Sgt James Borowski of the Grand County Sheriff's Department said hunter Barnes Wallace of Tabernash found the aircraft upside down atop a toppled tree in the Vasques Creek Drainage.

A six-state search ensued for a Beechcraft Baron when it vanished on a flight from Gallup, NM to Sturgis, SD, October 28, 1974. Killed in the crash were Dewey Rathke 38, and his brother-in-law Roger Hlavka 32, both from Sturgis. The Colorado Civil Air Patrol said Oliver Lane, an elk hunter from Odessa, TX., spotted the tail section of the air hearse wreckage Sunday, October 12th. The twin-engine plane transporting three bodies was the object of a year-long search.

Article in Pagosa Springs Newspaper

Long Missing Plane, Bodies Located
Pegosa Springs Colo*. (AP)*

An air-hearse missing for nearly a year with a crew of two and three bodies aboard has been located near here, the National Transportation Safety Board said today. There were no survivors of the crash. The wreckage of the plane was found by a hunter in the southwestern Colorado area on Wednesday. A spokesman for the board said the twin-engine was last heard from on a flight from Gallup, NM to Sturgis, SD. The plane was carrying victims of an auto/train accident back to South Dakota for burial.

The search for the plane was suspended last year when a five-foot snowfall hit the Pagosa Springs area but was resumed without success during the summer. The crew was identified as Dewey Rathke, 38, and Roger Hlavka, 32, both of Sturgis. The plane was located 18miles east of here in the mountains at elevation of 11,800 feet, a spokesman for Colorado Civil Air Patrol said. The CAP conducted the air search for the craft. Its tail section was spotted Oct. 12 by Oliver Lane of Odessa, Tex. who was hunting in the area. Officials took Lane over the area in a plane on Tuesday but could not find the craft. Only after continual searching was the wreckage spotted, visible for a brief time from the air.

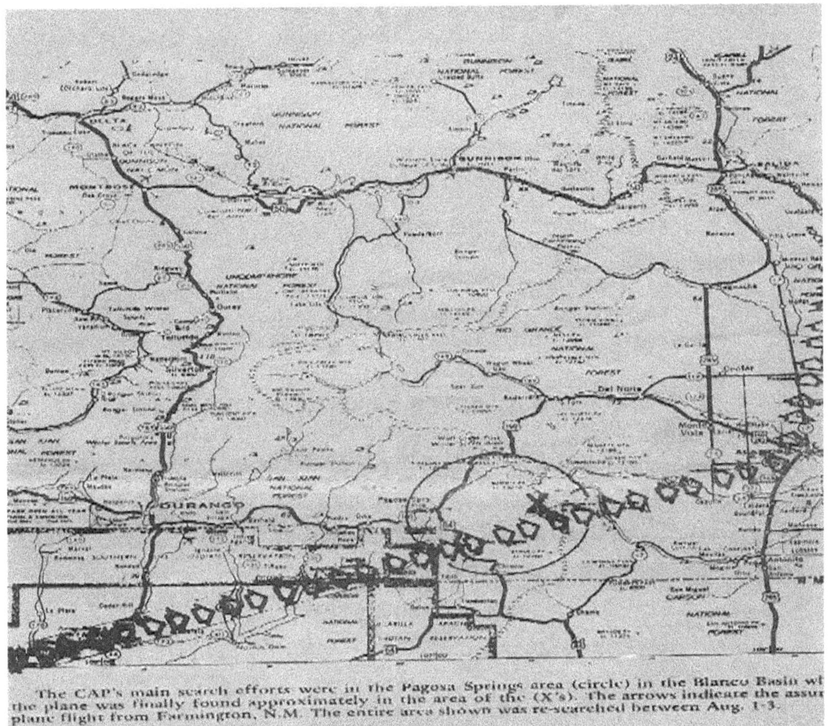

The CAP's main search efforts were in the Pagosa Springs area (circle) in the Blanco Basin wh the plane was finally found approximately in the area of the (X's). The arrows indicate the assur plane flight from Farmington, N.M. The entire area shown was re-searched between Aug. 1-3.

When speaking with FAA investigators I learned they had flown to the scene by helicopter; however, when they were trying to land, they began sliding down the mountainside and were forced to abandon their recovery attempt. Their final factual report compiled from information received from Judd Cooney provided the FAA with photos of the wreckage site and a detailed sketch marking the point of impact at estimated 11,000 feet. Over an area described as a steep one-hundred-yard decline at an estimated elevation of 9,800 feet, numbered X's identified findings: wings, engines, tail parts, seats, the cockpit, armrests, a Polaroid camera, wallet, and a girl's ring. An X next to the left of the fuselage and another to the right designated where the pilots were found, identified by descriptions of clothing.

It was noteworthy that photos show props of one engine pointing upward, undamaged; the other engine's props were twisted and mangled; evidence that one engine was not working, of which Mr. Hurkos was confident. This was verified several years later by our son, two of his friends and a helicopter pilot who went to the wreckage site. Peter was also correct when placing the airplane at an elevation of 9,800 feet; also, his sketch of the wreckage was almost identical to the photos taken!

NTSB Factual Aircraft Accident Report dated 10/75

*Location, 15 m. east southeast of Pegosa Springs, CO; Make, Beech 95-B-55 Air Hearse; Destroyed upon impact, transporting (3) bodies; Pilot in Command, Roger E. Hlavka, Hereford Rt. Sturgis, SD; Seat Occupied, unknown; Medical Cert, 2-5-74; Birth, 2/5/42; Pilot Time, this make, 30h; Night, 830hrs; Day, 6,000+ Inst, 145; Multi, 140; Total Flight **Time: 6,830 hrs+**; Passenger: Dewey Rathke, student pilot; Birth, 6/17/35 Hereford Rt., Sturgis SD; Pilot Time: 100hrs+; Seat Occupied, unknown; Cause: Undetermined*

There were no further investigations or assessments made by the FAA. The cause of the accident was listed as 'undetermined'. So, we were still left wondering, questioning why, how, and what really happened to cause the airplane to fail and the untimely deaths of Roger and Dewey. We do know that the airplane was running on one engine, that the pilots had turned back and were headed southeast, in the direction of Pagosa Springs Airport. According to speculative comments made by investigators, they had cleared one mountain ridge; and if merely one hundred feet higher, would have cleared the next one that took their lives. I had resigned myself to facing the fact that we would probably never know what really happened; needed to let go, but couldn't; I wasn't ready, didn't want to; nor capable of doing so, just yet!

CHAPTER 19

Saying Goodbye

The appropriate time had finally arrived to meet with Marty. Not knowing, is far worse than knowing; but now, it was absolute…we had proof, could make decisions. We first decided to hold private family services, until realizing that would be inappropriate. So many were involved, affected by the horrific tragedy which needed finalization and an opportunity to say goodbye. At Marty's recommendation, we planned a memorial service to be held in Grunwald Auditorium at the Sturgis High.

First, Marty would fly to Pagosa Springs and take care of whatever was needed to be done there; and honor our requests to bring back something that Wildlife Warden Judd Cooney and Bill Richardson from the District Attorney's Office had recovered at the wreckage sight. Upon returning, Marty gave us each an oblong manila envelope. In mine, were items retrieved from the cockpit: Roger's logbook, his billfold, a Masonic ring, and his large Black Hills Gold ring found embedded in the dashboard. I did not know or have ever known, what he brought back to Carol. Words could not express the gratitude I was feeling. My 'thank you' seemed so shallow, unworthy of how deeply grateful I was for all he had done. We shared a mutual hug, "See you Saturday Marty," I confirmed, "We'll be there early."

Joint services were held October 25th, 1975, three days short of when Roger and Dewey vanished one year earlier. Grunwald Auditorium overflowed with thoughtful, caring, wonderful friends, relatives, acquaintances, and many I did not know or recognize; many had to stand in the lobby. The families sat in front rows next to identical bronze coffins overlaid with flower sprays and banners reading: husband, father, son, brother, friend, pilot. Twelve close friends serving as pall bearers sat in the front row across from the families. Pastor Harold Fitch, First Methodist Church of Sturgis and Lutheran Pastor Rev. Paul Wendling of Rapid City officiated the memorial. The women's quartet from the Presbyterian Church sang beautiful hymns. The children, sitting silently with heads held high, holding the hands of aunts, uncles, grandpas, and grandmas who sprinkled amongst them, displayed admirable bravery and composure when saying goodbye to their fathers. Two special poems were shared.

<u>*A Child of Mine*</u>

I'll loan you for a little time, a child of mine he said; For you to love while living and mourn for when dead. It may be six or seven years or thirty-two or three.

But will you, until called back, take care of him for me? He'll bring charm to gladden you and should a stay be brief, you'll have smiles and memories as solace for your grief.

I cannot promise how long the stay, since all from earth return; but there are lessons taught down there I want each child to learn. I have looked this wide world over in my search for teachers true and from the throngs that crowd life's lanes, I have selected you. Now, will you give him all your love, nor think the labor vain;

nor hate me when he's called to come back home again.

I fancy what I heard him say, 'Dear Lord, thy will be done! For all the joy the child will bring a risk of grief you'll run.

I will shelter him with tenderness, with love when coming this way. Should the angels call for him much sooner than I planned,

be brave when bitter sadness comes, I'll comfort you, try to understand.

- Author Unknown

High Flight

I have slipped the surly bonds of Earth and danced the skies on laughter-silvered wings; Sunward I've climbed and joined the tumbling mirth of sun-split clouds and done a hundred things you have not dreamed of; wheeled, soared and swung, high in sunlit silence. Hovering there, I've chased the shouting wind along, and flung my eager craft through footless halls of air; up the long, delirious burning blue I've topped the wind- swept heights with easy grace where never lark, or ever eagle flew; and while with silent, lifting mind I've trod the high trespassed sanctity of space, put out my hand and touched the face of God.

by John Gillespie Magee, Jr

John Magee, Jr., an American pilot with the Royal Canadian Air Force in the Second World War went to Britain and flew in a Spitfire squadron. He was born in Shanghai, China in 1922, the son of missionary parents, Reverend and Mrs. John Gillespie Magee; his father was an American, his mother was originally a British citizen. In August or September 1941, Pilot Officer Magee composed 'High Flight' and sent a copy to his parents. A few months later, his Spitfire collided with another plane over England and was killed at the age of nineteen on December 11th, 1941, during a training flight.

(This heartfelt acknowledgment was placed in several newspapers locally, in Colorado & New Mexico)

"THANK YOU"

Sturgis, Hereford and Surrounding
Communities, Friends, Local Pilots, Ground
& Air Search Crews, CAP Units from NM,
CO, UT, SD, NE, WY, MN and NASA

Words are inadequate, incapable of expressing the deep gratitude we feel for your love, generosity, concern, kindness, compassion, and prayers. The strength we received from you made it possible to endure the past year.

We sincerely thank and appreciate everyone who reached out to us, and for everything you have done.

The continual efforts put forth by friends, acquaintances, and complete strangers was unbelievable! The volume of support received throughout the past year and at the memorial service for Roger and Dewey from so many of you was incredible, and very deeply appreciated.

We sincerely thank each one of
you! May God bless you!
The Rathke and Hlavka families

Those words hold true today, all these years later. I have not, nor will ever forget the goodness shown to us.

CHAPTER 20

Moving Forward/Quaal Ranch

Although dismal for a time, life did go on. I sold the house at the airport, dissolved the business, and purchased a home in Sturgis. When contacted by Rapid City First Federal Savings & Loan, I accepted a position as Loan Counselor with a team who opened the Sturgis Branch. Mick, the kids, and I were together often. A relationship developed, and my former employee and loyal friend, in July of '76, became my husband, who took on the responsibility as father of two pre-teen children.

Christian Michael *(Mick)*, and his four siblings Patsy, John, Laura, and Dorothy were born in Perkins County, South Dakota to Truman and Margaret Wammen Quaal. Margaret had attended Black Hills Normal, and taught school for five years prior to marrying. She became actively involved in the Strool community; took on leadership roles as President of Ladies Aid, Sunday School teacher, School Board clerk, Worthy Matron of Eastern Star and from all accounts was a wonderful lady and mother; had a cheerful disposition, gracious personality and was endeared by her many friends and all who knew her.

Quaal Ranch began as a homestead staked by Mick's grandparents. Annie Ramburg came to the area with two young boys and had a small one-room tar-papered wooden shack built, one mile north of the present- day ranch. John Quaal attended Lutheran Seminary and business school in Minnesota. He left there in 1903, first homesteading in Canada before settling at Strool in 1908, where he met Annie. They married on Valentine's Day in 1913. Their son Truman was born December 29th of that year.

John was very involved in the community, was a charter member of Homme Lutheran Church, served on township, school boards and twenty-four years as a Perkins County Commissioner. He, wife Annie and their son developed a ranching business, raising large herds of range horses and Black Angus cattle. Truman attended college in Minnesota until badly injured at the ranch. He eventually took over the large operation, had a deep benevolent interest in community affairs, followed in his father's footsteps and served as Perkins County Commissioner for twelve years.

Few families are spared some type of tragedy throughout their lifetime, but the Qualls have experienced more than their share. Truman's oldest half-brother, at age twelve, was helping with a corralled herd of wild horses by holding the rope lassoed around the neck of one. He was no contest for the strong, untamed equine that reared, spun around and took off dragging the youngster, who wouldn't or couldn't let go of the rope and tragically lost his life.

It was only days following the funeral of Truman's father when his wife, Margaret, became ill and was taken to Mayo Clinic at Rochester, Minnesota where she passed away at age forty-three. With a large ranch and five children to manage, Truman depended on help from relatives living in the Slim Buttes area near Sorum, South Dakota. With no children of their own, Uncle Buzz and Aunt Esther Wammen eagerly assumed the parenting of one-year-old Dorothy.

Uncle Vernon and Aunt Colleen Wammen willingly stepped up to assist the older Quaal children. Throughout the next school year, Colleen lived in Rapid City with them and her own four little ones during the week. On weekends they returned to their ranch homes to be with their fathers.

In time, Truman married Maxine Krause Sunding. She was a childless widow of many years, a former schoolteacher, resident of nearby Lodgepole; owner of Butterfield Grocery in Rapid City, and good friend of the Quaal family; who took on her role of ranch wife and mother, with grace and love! Truman's oldest son, at age twenty-one, and a fellow cadet at Wentworth Military Academy, were practicing spraying maneuvers when the wing of their plane clipped a treetop causing a crash, which took their young lives. The youngest of the family, while in her early twenties, when driving to work, hit ruts on a gravel road causing a serious accident. Since then, she has been confined to a wheelchair as a quadriplegic, but continues to drive her custom-built van, and efficiently manages her home in Sturgis. Dorothy, a true role model, is retired after working at Ft. Meade Veterans Hospital for several years.

After graduating from Rapid City Central High School, Mick attended the School of Mines for one year before being drafted into the Army in '66. He was stationed in the states at Ft. Bliss, Texas, Ft. Huachuca, Arizona where he received teletype training, transferred to Gordon, Georgia then Ft. Riley, Kansas. He was serving as company clerk, Sgt. E5 in Vietnam, when following the death of his brother; was granted a *hardship discharge* to assist his father on their large cattle ranch, and vast acreages of farmland, at Quaal Ranch; and attended Black Hills College, Spearfish, SD, where he earned his Business Degree.

When visiting Mick at the ranch for the first time, I rolled into the small rural village of Prairie City, South Dakota to take a quick tour before continuing a few miles south to what was to become the kids' and my new home. The small town is located between Buffalo and Bison, South Dakota on Hwy 20, near what was Old Strool, famous for their State Championship Baseball Team.

South of the highway was a café and bar, owned and operated by Clare John, a wonderful cook, mother, grandmother, widow *and* first female pilot in the area. During the blizzard of '49, she and her 'well-known 'barn stormer' husband Ike John; dropped food and other much needed supplies by air, to homes and ranches throughout the county, when all roads were blocked and impassable due to deep mountains of drifted snow.

Strool Oil, a maintenance shop and gas station operated by Orville and Eileen Tenold, and the Post Office managed by Postmaster Tom Haney, shared a large building located one block east. Tom and wife Winnie, who became two of my dearest friends; are on my list of the nicest people known! There were two churches, a schoolhouse, and a few residential homes. North of the highway, Keith Carr & Company operated an excavation business, digging dams throughout the county and beyond! A small trailer court was somewhat hidden behind a large wooden building which, at one time, was an active feed and seed business.

Jeannette Matson Sparks was the first person I met when stopping at Matson's Store, operated by her and husband Jim; established by Jeanette's parents, Frank and Isobel Matson. I introduced myself and expressed my excitement that groceries would be available so close by. During our conversation that pursued, she was somewhat taken back at my announcement. It seemed her lifetime friend, Mick; being the secretive bachelor he was, had failed to make it known that he was about to be married!

Our wedding was held on July 31, '76 at the First United Methodist Church in Sturgis with my children standing beside us. Close friends and family joined us at my home for the reception. I quit my job at First Federal S&L as VP Asst and Loan Counselor and sold our Sturgis house. Shortly, the kids and I moved north to vast ranch lands in Perkins County…a big change from tall Jack Pines and Black Hills Spruce.

Quaal Ranch~

Our home, built in '54, was a large, attractive, comfortable, four bedroom, two bathrooms three-story brick house; with stairways leading up to bedrooms and down to a large pantry area and rec room, where the pool table, piano and craft room provided fun, entertaining times. Activities such as church pianist, teaching piano, directing Bison Jr. Miss programs, and raising miniature horses; kept me occupied!

Adapting to my new life was easy. It took a bit of getting used to driving everywhere; but that comes with country living. I soon became involved in the community, as Church pianist, joined Ladies Aid, Delta Kappa Sorority, Eastern Star and a Bowling League in Bison; and developed a homebased business, Quaalarts offering handcrafted home décor and Hardley Hogs, oven-baked clay sculptures of little pigs dressed like '*biker dudes*. I peddled my goods in booths at craft fairs, including the Sturgis Motorcycle Rally and popular Festival of Arts, a huge event held each summer in Spearfish.

My in-laws, Truman and Maxine were wonderful, and very accepting of their new daughter-in-law and instant grandchildren. They had a home in Rapid City, where Truman spent most of his time. Mick assumed responsibility of operating the ranch, made needed improvements, built sturdy metal corrals at the barn and branding shed, and had a large new Morton building erected as his shop. He kept the road leading into the ranch maintained and repaved; reinsulated, remodeled the upstairs, re-sided the house with steel siding and added a deck to the house; where we and neighbors enjoyed many outdoor barbecues, and lively jam sessions! Mick dismantled the deteriorating homestead shack, salvaged the weathered boards and we used them to decorate one wall of our rec room.

When Truman made his weekly trip to the ranch, he occupied the bunkhouse and every morning, he and I shared coffee and many memorable conversations at the kitchen table. He was one of the nicest gentlemen I ever knew, was easy-going, highly respected by everyone who knew him. After Mick and I married, and I became friends with neighbors, several openly shared that Truman had helped them out financially and with whatever else was needed.

After learning he was to be grandpa again, we took his pickup to an old sheep shed and cleared a path through heaping piles of dusty stuff to the rear of the rickety wooden building. There he retrieved an old antique rocking chair. It was then he shared the history behind the beautiful piece of oak furniture in which he was nursed and rocked to sleep, as were his children. He thought it only fitting that the next generation of Quaal babies should experience the same pleasures. Truman took the curved-arm rocker with him that day and returned it beautifully restored, before the birth of Stacy. Kelly, our second daughter was born two years later. The historical rocker was put to good use!

Our two oldest children attended school in Prairie City and Bison for a year; then lived with grandparents until graduating from Sturgis High School. Occasionally, they brought a friend with them when returning to the ranch, which is always fun for a 'city kid' to get a 'taste of country'. The younger girls completed most of their elementary schooling in Prairie City. When entering Jr. High and High School, we purchased

a townhouse in Spearfish where they completed their secondary education, while I held daycare, taught piano and enrolled in college music courses. The girls were active in sports and extracurricular activities, which often were held on weekends. When we were unable to go home to the ranch, Mick joined us in town.

Summers at the ranch were most memorable when hosting social events, barbecues, and jam sessions. It was a wonderful place to raise our children, who all gained hands-on experience swathing, mowing, operating farm machinery, driving trucks, raising livestock, caring for animals, and branding cattle. It was especially fun for the kids when Lloyd, Arnita and son Ronnie Weber, longtime family friends from Lone Wolf, Oklahoma returned for harvest …with their crew of teenage boys, who often hung out at our house!

CHAPTER 21

Present Times

In 2001, Quaal Ranch, Inc. was purchased by South Dakota Schools and Public Lands. We sized down on a ranch north of Sundance, Wyoming, where Mick raised longhorn cattle and assisted friend Larry Carr with retrieving and transporting wrecked railroad cars, in need of repair. He has been a member of Masonic Lodge and Naja Shriners since age twenty-one and served several years on the High Plains Heritage Museum Board at Spearfish, SD, which his father was instrumental in establishing. He enjoys spending time at Sturgis Airport flying his plane, hanging out with fellow pilots and the Burnham boys, Scot and Roger. Both are airplane mechanics as was their father Jerry, who passed away in 2016. At that time, Roger took on the responsibility as operator of the privately owned Aviation Maintenance and Repair business established by their father; and serves as Sturgis Airport Manager as well.

Our oldest daughter, a graduate of Oklahoma State University, received a Juris Doctorate from University of Tulsa; practiced law and lived there with her husband and two daughters, for several years before moving closer to home. Lorie is service-oriented and takes on leadership roles in community affairs and organizations in addition to operating her business, Black Hills Law and Mediation in Rapid City, South Dakota. Her oldest daughter served two years with the Peace Corp in Africa, taught English in Japan, and presently works with a lobbyist attorney in Tokyo. Her youngest daughter earned a master's degree in environmental management and is an

Urban Forestry Associate in Tulsa, Oklahoma with a non-profit organization, 'Up with Trees'.

Son Ed, following high school, attended the Institute of Art and Design in Minneapolis; but disillusioned when having to take *'art history'* classes; rather than learning *'hands on'* sculpting techniques! When returning home, he assisted local Sturgis sculptor, Dale Lamphere *(who once told me my son, was a 'sculpting genius')*. Ed moved to Loveland, CO where he assisted well-known sculptor George Lundeen. By teaching sculpting classes, competing in art shows, and entering Calls for Artists contests; he soon built up a reputation for his intricately detailed, life-size figurative bronze artworks. Some of these statues include George Washington and Oneida Mother of the Tribe at Smithsonian's National Museum for the American Indian; Helen Keller located at Statuary Hall, Washington, DC; Louie Armstrong playing his trumpet, at New Orleans; and several other life-size figures located throughout St. George, Utah including a well-known doctor outside the hospital; and Indians on wild horses galloping in a roundabout.

Local statues include Presidents Nixon, Jefferson, Bush, FDR, and Van Buren on Rapid City's downtown street corners; Colonel Sturgis on horseback with two children feeding his horse apples near Fort Meade, SD; Sundance Kid peering from a jail cell at the Sundance, Wyoming Courthouse; and the popular outdoor piece featuring an elderly lady reading to children on a bench at Rapid City Public Library. He is presently working with the Deadwood Arts Council, creating statues of historical characters for Main Street corners. He has one child, Tia Bella whom he claims as his best work of art, a beautiful young lady, a budding artist in her own right, works fulltime, and operates her online business. She lives in St. George, Utah, where our son made his home for many years, and resided in Florida for a while before moving to Deadwood.

After graduating from Spearfish High School, our second daughter Stacy, obtained a Radiology Degree from Presentation College in Aberdeen, South Dakota, worked at the Denver Trauma Center before returning home, and at times works on call locally. She and her two amazing, talented and athletic daughters are our closest neighbors at the ranch, just a few steps away! Karly currently attends Sundance High. Rylie, a recent graduate from there; has enrolled in college at Billings, Montana.

Our youngest daughter Kelly: also a graduate of Spearfish High School attended Concordia College in Moorhead, Minnesota then received a Doctorate in Physical/Occupational Therapy from the University of St Augustine, Florida, and presently practices in Houston. She has a handsome nine-year-old, our only grandson; a very pleasant young man, actively involved in sports.

As for me, having lived my entire life either on the prairies or in the Black Hills of South Dakota and Wyoming, and traveled in several foreign countries; I have no desire to live anywhere else but here in the greatest country of all, and plan to stay put in Spearfish, SD. Recently, there have been big changes in my life. After forty-five years of marriage, Mick and I divorced, but remain amiable. That doesn't seem to make much sense, but *'it'* happens! Then, after working for many years as Senior Center Director, Activity Director at Long Term Care, Assisted Living facilities and as a Residential Caregiver; I retired and have joined up as pianist with a Dixieland band, appropriately called "The Medicares"; and *tickle the ivories* with a banjo pick'n friend. Both groups provide entertainment at senior centers, residential facilities, assisted livings, nursing homes, parties and special events.

My plans are to *'keep-on-keeping-on'* as long as my *'can-do'* keeps up with my *'want-to'*... continue to play piano, write children stories, poems, take good care of my two cuddly housecats, spend more time with friends, daughter and sister-in-law in Rapid City; hopefully visit my son and grandchildren out-of-state; and work sudoku... *which is supposed to keep my brain awake!*

CHAPTER 22

Making of the Book

When taking on the endeavor, which I put upon myself; I found it to be more difficult than expected and took much longer than planned. Raw emotions thought to be long-since buried, emerged each time when retrieving a familiar brown cardboard box containing search details. To ward off a full-fledged anxiety attack, I deliberately refrained from working on my project in the fall, which delayed things. When I did delve back into the worst year of my life; the time spent sorting, organizing, and summarizing was kept to a minimum. The undertaking was involved, but emotions were waning with the passing of each October. However, the completion of my book was delayed, when parents' health began failing and took on the duty as their personal caregiver. Dad had the foresight, to attach a small apartment on the west end of their home. That is where I resided, for the last few years of their lives.

My father, following several months of suffering from colon cancer, lost his hard-fought battle on October 30th, 2006. Almost one year to the day, my mother experienced the first of several stem cell strokes which continued until her passing on January 30th, 2008. They were my constants, the best parents anyone could ever ask for; were patient with me during the awkward teenage years, supportive as a wife, mother; later, as a young widow and second marriage.

The autumn following my mother's death, was strangely different. It was a major turning point. I woke early on the dreaded October day, permanently imbedded within my soul, with intense thoughts of my mother. "Time to get up, Jean Ann, time to get going" she would say. "We have things to do!"

With whistling wind and dried leaves persistently rapping at my bedroom window, thoughts of staying forever snuggled beneath the warmth of a fluffy down-filled comforter, were short-lived. The intermittent buzzing of my alarm added to the early morning annoyances. Reluctantly, I exited my protective safety zone and was led to the kitchen by the aroma of fresh brewing coffee.

My thoughts remained with mom to the degree that I could feel her presence. She was an avid coffee drinker, the stronger the better; and was the only liquid, other than water, that she consumed. She used to tell me as a child that if I drank coffee, someday the back of my ears would turn black. That kept me away from the stuff for a long time!

Open blinds perfectly framed the kitchen window displaying a wondrous, spectacular scene of soft peach, blues, and pinks streaking through billowing puffy clouds hovering above distant hills to the east. Patches of brilliant and scorching reds enhanced the rolling landscape of variegated greens. The view was breathtaking, unlike any before!

The inspirational masterpiece brought about a calmness but generated a sense of strength. Its persuasive message indisputably commanded that I embrace rather than deny, the power of autumn's colorful pallet; and decided to focus my attention on what had been in the making for far too many years!

Challenged by nature, rejuvenated, and encouraged by my mother's words, I retrieved the dusty cardboard box from safekeeping and removed a large manila envelope labeled 'The Search'. It was well into the night when placing it back into the box, almost completed. After a few more all-night sessions, including several spells of writer's block, I felt somewhat satisfied with what I hoped would be a finalized manuscript. Introducing family histories, stories of predecessors, happy times, and excerpts from my childhood, lightened the solemn nature of my writing. When sharing yesteryears, it became easier, was therapeutic and my journal of sorts gradually transformed into an autobiography memoir, rather than a compilation of grim search details. When learning about Bear Lodge Writers, I met with a group of amateur and seasoned authors to have them critique my writing. They were extremely helpful when sharing suggestions, writing techniques, and tips on marketing and publishing. Other than printing a few copies for those intended, I had no plans of sharing our sensitive and painful experience with the public; the media had shared enough information. Although reports widely publicized in newspapers, tv, and radio broadcasts from South Dakota to Colorado were accurate and factually correct; I realized a personal accounting of the search would dispel myths, mistruths, and falsehoods that had circulated locally. I was encouraged by friends and fellow writers that our story should be told; others who have experienced similar situations might find it beneficial.

After receiving the necessary permissions and researching extensively online, I submitted several queries to publishers. Pleasantly surprised when receiving positive feedback and offers to publish, I began editing and re-editing until I was prepared to go forth with my book. Other published works are an illustrated children's book entitled *"If Roosters Crow,"* Outskirts Press, 2001 and an original poem *"Woodland Elves"* included in "America at the Millennium, The Best Poems and Poets of the 20th Century," Watermark Press, 2000. A book based on that poem, *'Where Woodland Elves and Fairies Bound'* features original scenic photos and illustrations where mystical creatures are found; a fantasy tale *'Forever Never Everland'*, where *'pretending'* and *'wishing'* works; as well as several other original poems, remain unpublished.

Footnotes

This book was written in remembrance of Roger Hlavka and Dewey Rathke, with special acknowledgement and gratitude to Marty Jolly, Judd Cooney, Mr. Oliver Lane, SD Senator Abourezk, Peter Hurkos; and all state and federal aviation agencies involved throughout the search.

In Chapter VI, I noted having other visitations from Roger. It was shortly after remarrying, when he appeared briefly above the foot of my bed.

Everything was the same as previous visits. The room was darkened, except for moonlight shining through an open window. His gradual appearance was hazy and subtle. There was no verbal communication. Looking downward, he flashed his big wide toothy smile then slowly faded away. That was his final visitation!

<u>Credits</u>

Meade County History, Vol 1, 19 Mary Alice McFarland
Faith County1910-60 Mary Ann Hlavka George Hlavka
Sally Hlavka

<u>Abbreviations</u>

CAP (Civil Air Patrol)
DOT (Dept of Transportation)
ELT (Emergency Locator Transmitter) ETA (Estimated Time of Arrival)
FAA (Federal Aviation Administration) FBO (Fixed Base Operation)
FSS (Flight Service Station) IFR(Instrumental Flight Rules)
NATSB (National Aviation Transportation Safety Board) VAH (Veterans Administration Hospital)
VFR (Visual Flight Rule) VOR(Visual Omni Range)

www.ingramcontent.com/pod-product-compliance
Lightning Source LLC
Chambersburg PA
CBHW040831010826
48978CB00012BB/704